Kathryn's heart lodged in her throat

Across the room she spotted Curt...waiting for her.

His cocky gaze was an indecent assault on her senses. He gave her a slow, satisfied perusal, a look that raised Kathryn's temperature by several degrees. Every exposed inch of her skin flushed, along with a fair amount of flesh duly hidden beneath fabric.

The maddening millionaire didn't try to disguise his intentions. The glint in his eye was there for anyone to see. It said the self-assured, world-class womanizer was willing to play any game Kathryn chose.

But eventually she'd lose.

And he'd be around to collect the prize.

Her!

ABOUT THE AUTHOR

Charlotte Maclay was delighted when her editor asked her to write the first book in the For Richer, For Poorer promotion. When a gorgeous playboy millionaire sets his sights on the persnickety—and very proper—Ms. Prim, the result is a delightful tale of a woman who pretends to want nothing, but ends up with everything!

Charlotte has had bits and pieces of stories running through her head for as long as she can remember. Until recently, however, she concentrated her writing in the nonfiction area. But in her imagination, she's always produced stories of romance, which she is now delighted to share with her readers. Charlotte lives in Southern California with her husband, Chuck, and their very spoiled cat, Patches.

Books by Charlotte Maclay

HARLEQUIN AMERICAN ROMANCE

474—THE VILLAIN'S LADY
488—A GHOSTLY AFFAIR
503—ELUSIVE TREASURE
532—MICHAEL'S MAGIC
537—THE KIDNAPPED BRIDE

CHARLOTTE MACLAY

HOW TO MARRY A MILLIONAIRE

Harlequin Books

TORONTO • NEW YORK • LONDON
AMSTERDAM • PARIS • SYDNEY • HAMBURG
STOCKHOLM • ATHENS • TOKYO • MILAN
MADRID • WARSAW • BUDAPEST • AUCKLAND

ISBN 0-373-16566-8

HOW TO MARRY A MILLIONAIRE

Copyright © 1995 by Charlotte Lobb.

Chapter One

"No, don't tell him I called," she said, her voice catching. "I'll get back to you later."

Hand trembling, Kathryn Prim hung up the phone on her desk and used a tissue to wipe a tear from her eye. That had been the most difficult call of her life . . . one that was long overdue.

Before she could draw a shaky breath, a large, very masculine hand closed firmly over her shoulder.

Kathryn screamed.

"Hey, it's all right, pretty lady. You probably should have dumped the bum years ago."

Heart thundering, Kathryn swiveled in her chair, shifting her gaze from the man's powerful hand to the showy silver belt buckle at his tapered waist, up past a worn leather jacket that tugged across broad shoulders, to a pair of blue-green eyes that smiled down at her. Sweat marks from the motorcycle helmet he carried tucked under his arm darkened the waves of his cinnamon brown hair. Somebody must have left the office door unlocked after-hours, she swiftly concluded, and this guy was a late special messenger with papers for her attorney boss, Tom Weston.

She hoped.

Gathering herself, she said, "I didn't hear you come in."

"No problem." As though he owned the place, he pulled up her office mate's chair, sat down and extended his jeans-clad legs, crossing one booted foot over the other. The soles were almost worn through. As he leaned back, the chair squeaked under his weight—a hundred ninety pounds of serious masculinity. "The way I see it, the guy must be nuts to let you go. Anybody can see you're a knockout. The pick of this year's crop. Why, you probably have half the men in town waiting in line to ask you out."

Not likely, and even the thought wasn't particularly flattering. Kathryn made it a point to avoid that kind of a reputation. "I have no idea what you're talking about."

"That phone call. I came in and there you were, crying..." He leaned toward her, a little too close for comfort—bringing with him the enticing scent of spicy after-shave—and rested his elbows on his knees. His perusal was disturbingly intimate, skimming across her hair, which she wore tied back in a neat bun, then lingering an extra moment on the all-too-rapid rise and fall of her breasts beneath her tailored blouse.

As he shifted the helmet, she noticed a fine smattering of light brown hair on the backs of his hands, and long, tapered fingers. His fingernails were surprisingly well-trimmed and manicured compared to the casual way he was dressed. "You weren't talking to your boyfriend?" he asked.

"No. My sister, Alice." It had taken Kathryn weeks to build up the courage to make that single call, which she was in no mood to discuss with anyone. "I haven't spoken with her in years. Though I really don't see that it's any business of yours."

He frowned, though not in a way that suggested he was in the least put off by her statement. "Then you didn't just get dumped?"

"It hardly seems possible since I don't even have a boyfriend."

"Well, hallelujah!" His broad grin creased both of his cheeks in a totally infectious way. "That leaves the field clear for me."

She stifled a responding smile. This guy certainly didn't let any grass grow under his feet. He'd probably developed his *winning* technique at the local singles' bar. "Mr....I'm afraid I didn't get your name?"

"Curt Creighton, bachelor millionaire at your service, ma'am." He gave her another one of those disarming smiles that begged for company.

She resisted...barely. "Mr. Creighton, I don't happen to be in the market for a bachelor millionaire right now. But if you're here to deliver some papers to my employer, Mr. Weston, or to one of the other attorneys, I'd be happy to sign for them.''

His gaze flicked to the nameplate on the side of her desk that identified her as a paralegal, then back again. "Please don't reject me, Katie, my girl."

She winced at the use of the nickname that brought back nothing but bad memories. "I prefer *Ms. Prim,* if you don't mind."

His lips twitched and he cocked an amused eyebrow.

"And I've heard all the jokes, so don't bother."

"Yes, ma'am, whatever you say...Ms. Prim." He said her name slowly, letting the final syllable slip through his lips in a slow, sensual breath. "But you see, when a beautiful woman turns me down, particularly one who's been crying, I view it as a challenge to bring a little happiness into her life again."

"Namely you?"

He shrugged and amused crinkles formed at the corners of his eyes. "Surely you don't doubt I could bring a smile to your lovely lips."

She stood and narrowed her gaze. The look would have cowed a lesser man. It didn't budge this guy— not an inch. Studying him again, she belatedly noted a stubborn set to his jaw, a never-say-never glint in his eye. Smiling or not, the man was a predator at heart. The realization sent an anxious feeling burrowing into the back of her skull.

"I *doubt* you'll have the opportunity to do anything regarding my lips." Kathryn sensed that if she gave Curt Creighton a chance, his overpowering personality and his damnably attractive grin might well get him more than simply a smile. Forget that as a messenger he probably didn't have but a little loose change in his pocket, wild story about millions to the contrary. She'd vowed when she left home at age seventeen she'd never trust a man again. Rich or poor. For twelve years she'd kept that promise... mostly by avoiding temptation. She wasn't about to change her modus operandi now.

He rose slowly from the chair, finally standing full height, his chin level with the top of her head. "That definitely sounds like a challenge, Ms. Prim."

His soft, intimate tone skidded along her spine. She fought the sensation, watching with a degree of anxiety as he casually slid his hand inside his jacket.

"Do you prefer swords or pistols at dawn?" he asked, then cocked a single brown eyebrow. "Or more appropriately, roses or diamonds at dusk?"

"I prefer you leave. Now." She hated the husky, hesitant note in her voice.

From under his jacket he produced a large, brown envelope and handed it to her. "Tell Tom I'll see him in the morning. I'll see you then, too."

In the worst way Kathryn wanted to deny the possibility. "Are you a... client?" On a first-name basis with the boss?

"When some woman tries to nail me with a negligence suit, I am. The rest of the time I'm an ol' college buddy."

"I see."

"The lady claims she hurt her back when she fell out of my bed."

Kathryn raised her eyebrows. *It figured.*

"Well, not exactly *my* bed," he continued. "The one in the guest bedroom."

Given Curt's athletic appearance and his cavalier attitude, she doubted the distinction had much legal merit. "I'll see Mr. Weston gets the information."

"I'd appreciate it." He took a couple of steps toward the doorway, just enough to give Kathryn some sense of relief, then turned back. "You planning to close up shop soon?"

"In a minute."

"Good. I'll wait for you."

"You really don't have to do that, Mr. Creighton."

"Curt," he corrected with easy insistence. "It's after dark and the building is empty. I don't want you riding down in the elevator all alone. That's not a good idea in a city like Los Angeles."

"I've been managing alone for years, thank you."

"Ah. I suppose you've had one of those self-defense courses. Waste of time with a determined mugger."

Kathryn felt the guilty heat of a flush creep up her neck. She'd often thought much the same herself. "I also used to be on the high-school track team, if that reassures you."

"Nope. I'll just wait." He leaned against the doorjamb and folded his arms across his chest, his helmet dangling from one hand.

Among assorted attributes, stubbornness appeared to be a dominant characteristic in males, she concluded, not for the first time. It didn't disturb her greatly. She could be pretty obstinate herself. "If you'll wait in the reception area, I'll be right there."

When he left, she quickly put away the papers on her desk, delivered the envelope to Tom's office and locked all of the inner doors. Then she slipped out the private entrance. When she got downstairs, she'd ask the security guard to make sure Mr. Creighton had left the office. Meanwhile, she'd be safely on her way.

She walked resolutely down the carpeted hallway. Rounding the corner to the elevators, she stopped dead in her tracks.

"Ready to go?" Curt asked with the casual ease of a man who always got his way. He had already pushed the button and had the open elevator waiting for them.

Stepping inside, she faked a weak smile, hoping she wasn't making a serious mistake. She carefully placed herself next to the control panel, her finger practically resting on the emergency bell. In the musty confines of the elevator she easily caught the appealing scent of his after-shave. He was, after all, a client of the firm and one of Tom Weston's friends. Or so he said.

Except for the odd curl of warmth in her midsection generated by Curt's amused expression, the ride down to the first floor was uneventful. She watched with a certain amount of relief, however, as the doors parted.

Before she could step from the elevator, Curt right beside her, the brilliant flash of a camera struck her in the face, not once, but twice, in quick succession. Purple spots appeared before her eyes.

"Thanks, Mr. Creighton," the photographer called, dashing toward the exit.

"Damn," Curt muttered under his breath.

Blinking, Kathryn asked, "What the hell was that all about?"

"The paparazzi. Yellow-rag photographers and journalists follow me around all the time." He slipped his arm around her waist in a thoroughly proprietary gesture, finally escorting her out of the elevator. "Sorry about that. I thought I'd lost them on my motorcycle."

"Why on earth would they want to..." Her jaw dropped open. Curt Creighton, heir to the Creighton fortunes, millionaire playboy and the owner of Seduction Incorporated—a man who was the object of more gossip than Princess Di. My God, she'd never made the connection...

She nearly ran to her car, though Curt, with his long-legged strides, had no trouble keeping up with her. Kathryn didn't want anything to do with a guy who was the center of so much attention. Privacy.

Nobody snooping into her personal affairs. That's the way she lived her life.

Her hand shook as she unlocked the car door, and her knees felt a little wobbly as she slid into the driver's seat. It had been bad enough as a teenager to know everyone in town knew what she was up to; it would mean even more misery to have the entire world aware of her least little indiscretion.

CURT WATCHED KATHRYN drive her VW Rabbit out of the nearly empty underground parking lot. The rough sound of the engine echoed through the concrete structure as he tugged on his helmet. He hadn't been kidding when he'd called her a pretty lady. Her hair was a striking shade of blond, with just a hint of strawberry and enough natural curl so the strands gave the impression they were struggling to escape the severe hairdo they were forced to endure. Her tasteful makeup didn't quite cover a light sprinkling of freckles across her nose and cheeks.

Her figure was good, too, and so were her legs, what he'd seen of them when her skirt rode up a bit as she slid into her car.

Of course, a woman in tears had always been his weakness. At least, according to his sister, Lucy, that was true.

Kathryn had something else going for her, though. Sadness lingered in her melt-your-heart hazel eyes even when she was trying to be tough. He suspected that beneath her tailored clothes, she was trying to hide something—from herself as much as anyone else. Something more than a few freckles. Maybe a big-time capacity to care, he mused as he tightened the helmet strap under his chin. An admirable trait that could get a woman into a whole lot of trouble if she came up against the wrong guy.

And her voice. If rose petals could speak, they'd sound like Kathryn Prim—soft and velvety.

He twisted the ignition key of the Harley and felt the power rise beneath him. Tomorrow, he promised himself, he'd find an opportunity to get to know Kathryn a little bit better.

Smiling from behind the tinted visor, he wondered if she was as straitlaced as her last name implied. Or if with the proper tutelage she could be thoroughly shameless.

KATHRYN PARKED IN FRONT of her apartment house, a three-story stucco building a block off of Wilshire Boulevard. The Santa Monica neighborhood still had a certain amount of charm despite its aging veneer. As she eased out of the car, she discovered every muscle in her body ached. A definite sign of stress.

Before she reached the building's entrance, her favorite neighbor greeted her on the sidewalk with a cheery, "Hello, my little chickadee. It appears you've had a hard day."

She smiled in spite of herself. The guy must be psychic. "Hello, Rudy. How ever did you guess?"

"Ah, you forget, *mon amie,* I am an actor, a master of body language." The wiry octogenarian hadn't had a part in twenty years . . . nor had he forgotten a single line he'd ever spoken on camera. "I see how your shoulders are hunched and the creases that mar your lovely forehead."

Evidently the knot in Kathryn's stomach wasn't visible. Building up enough courage to call her kid sister for the first time in twelve years had generated a whole lot of anxiety. Somehow Kathryn had known Alice would still be living in the small farming community in central California where they grew up. Kathryn simply hoped her sister would keep her word not to tell their father she'd called. She wasn't quite ready to face that particular challenge just yet.

"It was a long day," she hedged, unwilling to talk about the whole rash of stressful experiences she'd had in the past hour or so.

"It is more than that, my darling," Rudy insisted, adjusting the jaunty angle of his beret on his full head of white hair. "Perhaps you are ill? Your face appears flushed."

"I'm fine. Really." Responsibility for her accelerated heartbeat and the continued rapid flow of blood through her veins could be laid right at the feet of Curt Creighton. She could have handled him if he'd only been a lothario in messenger's garb. Certainly she'd had plenty of experience dodging unwelcome advances.

"You vant already to come up to my apartment," Rudy offered, slipping into one of the many characters in his repertoire. He had an amazing facility to imitate voices and accents. "I made chicken soup like my mother—"

"No, thanks. I'll zap something in the microwave. I've got a lot of studying to do." She tried to slip past him on the walkway, but he didn't give an inch.

"Bah. You study too hard. You should be having fun. Going to parties." He gestured expansively, his full shirtsleeves creating their own breeze. "You should be finding a man."

This evening a man had found her. A man she sensed was very dangerous....and possibly determined. "I'm getting a law degree, Rudy. Going to night school two evenings a week means a lot of work." Considering the couple of times a week she tried to get to the gym for a jazzercise workout, there were few leisure moments in her life, and she liked it that way.

"But it is so boring, *chérie.*"

"Yes. I know." She outmaneuvered him and hurried up the steps. She *was* boring. Intentionally so. Once the talk of the town, albeit a small town, she'd vowed never to let that happen again.

Now some jerk-face photographer might be planning to plaster her picture across a national tabloid, with who knew what kind of a suggestive headline, and link her name with that of Curt Creighton. According to the press, he was a world-class womanizer. His face—and often his muscular physique—hit the grocery store tabloids with considerable regularity, usually with a woman at his side wearing a skimpy swimsuit that revealed more than it hid. Apparently the man spent a great deal of time with female companions, lounging around the heart-shaped pool at his Hollywood Hills mansion.

Not that Kathryn had read any of the articles about the guy. But the headlines were enough to bring a blush to the cheeks of even an experienced woman.

He was skilled in the art of flirtation, she'd give him that. Evidently far more skilled than she was at keeping her reactions under control. He had an uncanny knack of getting too close, of entering a woman's private space to make her think about hot, sweaty bodies and long, languorous nights. Forbidden thoughts she'd discarded years ago.

The whole experience had been enough to give her a migraine—a nasty one that blurred her vision as she slid her key into the apartment lock.

She could only hope both the photographer and Curt Creighton would lose interest in her in a hurry. After all, she was too overdressed to make a big splash on the front page of a tabloid, and far too uncooperative for a man like Creighton.

After changing into comfortable slacks and a warm sweater against the chill of an autumn evening, she took her microwaved dinner into the second bedroom. Like the rest of the small apartment, everything in her office was orderly. Books were lined on bookshelves and arranged alphabetically by author for fiction, by subject for nonfiction, and there was a special section for her textbooks. Three carefully sharpened pencils lay in a neat row on the right-hand side of the walnut desk, and a crooked-neck lamp lit a spotless mock-leather desk pad. At some intuitive level she admitted her fetish for being organized was an effort to keep her emotions as well ordered as her professional life. Surely no one could criticize her subconscious motives.

Settling herself at the desk, she opened a casebook on torts and flipped through the pages to a section on contributory negligence. A little smile played at the corners of her lips.

That must have been quite a night to remember if Curt and his plaintiff lady friend had fallen out of bed. As strictly an academic exercise, she wondered who would be considered at fault? Of course, she mused, as defense attorneys they could do a re-creation of the event to demonstrate shared responsibility. A jury would love that. As Tom Weston's assistant, Kathryn would no doubt be assigned to act as the injured woman, lying in bed with Curt, having him hold her up close to his muscular body, then kissing her with his sensuous lips, and finally...

She slammed the book shut.

Those kinds of thoughts were definitely not part of her homework. Perhaps for tonight she should concentrate on criminal law.

Chapter Two

Roses.

Buckets of them. On her desk. On top of the filing cabinet. Stuffed into the bookcase. Filling the room with a heady perfume and spilling out of Kathryn's office into the hallway of Weston, Lyman and Garcelli like a bright red carpet.

A color that no doubt matched the angry flush on her cheeks.

"I hope you like roses," said a baritone voice behind her. "I didn't have time to pick up any diamonds."

She whirled around and nailed Curt Creighton with a look meant to communicate her fury. His predatory grin and his chambray shirt, open at the collar to reveal an enticing tuft of cinnamon brown chest hair, did nothing to dissuade her.

"This is a business office." She added as much ice to her tone as she could manage, given the way her heart was thudding painfully against her ribs. "Not a florist shop...or a funeral parlor."

"I do believe you have a temper, Ms. Prim. Good for you."

"You have no right—"

"It was my pleasure, Ms. Prim." He gave her an arrogant dip of his head. "You're more than welcome."

"What will people think?" she protested between tight lips, glancing across the expanse of cubicles where secretaries and bookkeepers worked behind low partitions. More than one curious face peered back at her. "I don't even know you."

"I plan to rectify that oversight as soon as possible. Tonight at dinner seems like a good time to get started."

She sputtered. "Dinner? I'm not going anywhere with you."

"You have to eat. Everyone does." He cocked one eyebrow and shifted his gaze slowly, suggestively, over her slender figure, making Kathryn wish she were wearing a plastic garbage sack instead of a tailored suit with a tight-fitting skirt. "Of course, it doesn't look like you'd bankrupt me in that department." His gaze lifted again to meet hers, his eyes filled with wicked amusement. "You like continental or Mexican?"

"Neither." She stooped, picked up a dozen flowers and shoved them hard against his unyielding chest. "I want you to take these roses back to wherever you got them."

"I don't think they give refunds."

"Fine. Then make friends with somebody in a hospital. I don't want them and I don't want you harassing me."

"Harassing? Is that what I'm doing? And here I thought it was called courtship." He shook his head in mock confusion. "Guess I'll have to go back and read *that* book one more time."

He'd written the book, for heaven's sake! It was called Seduction Incorporated, a catalog service featuring every imaginable gift a man might purchase to seduce a woman—filmy negligees, extraordinary flowers like those filling her office, chocolates so rich just looking at the pictures added two inches to a woman's thighs, and exquisite, sultry perfumes for about a million dollars an ounce. Then came the diamonds and elegant cars, every display and gift carefully conceived to weaken a woman's resistance while, no doubt, making megabucks for Creighton Enterprises.

Kathryn would have popped her cork right then, except her employer appeared from out of his office.

"Hey, buddy, you giving my associate a hard time?" Smiling, Tom Weston extended his hand in friendly greeting.

Blowing out a sigh of relief, Kathryn let the tension ease from her shoulders and neck. Tom would get this Don Juan off her case. Her employer was a very serious guy, a bachelor who was as fully circumspect about his personal life as she. He'd put an end to Curt's disruptive behavior in a hurry.

"I'm as innocent as a little lamb," Curt said. "You know that."

Tom shifted an interested gaze into Kathryn's rose-filled office and back to Curt again. "I doubt Kathryn would believe that statement—even under oath—any more than I do." Laughing, he took his friend by the arm. "Come on into my office. We need to talk about this little difficulty you've gotten yourself into."

"Right you are." Before following Tom to his office, Curt leaned over the first partitioned cubicle and handed Marcy Higgins the roses Kathryn had shoved into his arms. "Here you go, sweetheart. Flowers for a lovely lady." He brushed his fingertips against her wrinkled cheek.

The gray-haired woman giggled her thanks.

Kathryn rolled her eyes. The man was an incorrigible flirt.

As Curt stepped into Tom's office, he glanced back at Kathryn and winked. "I'll check with you later about tonight."

Ignoring him, she turned away. "Don't bother," she muttered under her breath.

There was no way she could ignore the array of roses still filling her office, however, or the way Curt

Creighton left her feeling slightly breathless and oddly weak in the knees.

CURT MOVED with restless energy across Tom's office. Hands in his pockets, he stopped at the window and studied the curving view of Santa Monica Bay from his friend's twentieth-floor office. A brown smudge along the horizon marked the edge of the smog blown out to sea by a warm breeze from the desert.

"Tell me about her," he said.

"Kathryn? She's a damn good paralegal. She'll make a good attorney, too. We've already offered her a job when she passes the bar, which ought to be sometime next year."

"Ambitious lady. I like that." He also liked how she looked in her trim-fitting rust suit. The shade definitely accented the color of her hair, picking up the red highlights like heated sparks from a banked fire.

Tom cleared his throat and there was a shuffle of papers. "I think you ought to leave her alone."

Raising his eyebrows, Curt turned to his friend. Though both men were about thirty-five, they were physical opposites, Tom being lean and wiry, while Curt carried far more height and bulk. "Why? Last night when I brought those papers by, she claimed she wasn't involved with anyone right now."

"As far as I know, she hasn't had a serious relationship since she came to work for my father twelve years ago in the mail room."

"So? What's the problem?"

"None, as far as she's concerned. She's a very private person. Never talks about her personal life. Never shows up late for work, as though she's been out on the town, or brings a date to office parties. I just don't think she's your type."

"Why the heck not? Don't make me out to be some kind of an ogre."

"Come on, Curt. You live on the fast track."

"You know that's more publicity hype than fact. Besides, I've slowed down a whole lot in the past few years." If truth be known, he'd grown tired of the party scene. Maybe he was getting old. But he'd inherited a playboy image from his father along with the wealth that went with it. It made a certain amount of marketing sense to continue nurturing that image, or at least the PR folks at Creighton Enterprises seemed to think so.

Tom held up the copy of the lawsuit. "It doesn't look to me like you've slowed down much since we were in college. Not if there's any merit in—" he glanced at the plaintiff's name "—in Roslyn Kellogg's case."

"She fell out of bed, all right—she was pretty well soused that night, and maybe she even hurt her back. But I wasn't anywhere near her at the time. I heard her scream and went running into the guest bedroom to see what was the matter. I found her on the floor.''

"And she has a half-dozen witnesses who will testify that they discovered you, stark naked, holding her in your arms.''

"So I sleep in the buff and I didn't take time to put on my pants. There's no law against that.''

"Depends on who you're sleeping with, I guess, and how athletic your activities get.''

Curt paced across the plush carpeting, placed his hands on the back of one of the leather chairs facing Tom's oversize desk and squeezed hard enough to turn his knuckles white. "Roz is a kid. She can't be more than twenty-one. I gave her a roof over her head when she didn't have anyplace else to go, for God's sàke, and now she's trying to take advantage. I don't mind a little negative publicity once in a while, but I'll be damned if I'll let a woman take me to the cleaners just because she thinks I've got deep pockets.''

"You do.''

"Yeah, and it's your job to keep her greedy little hands out of 'em. Roz had started hanging around with a kind of sleazy character. Frankly, I think he may have put her up to this suing business.''

Tom speared his fingers through his blond, neatly combed hair. "I'll do the best I can, but I don't think it's going to be easy. If this is a scam, you're a ready-made victim.''

"Tell me about it," Curt agreed with a grim twist of his lips. Over the years, Creighton Enterprises had paid a fortune to fight frivolous suits. It was a matter of principle not to pay out a dime unless the organization, or the individual involved, really did have legitimate liability. Recently, the legal firm they'd retained for years hadn't been producing. Curt had decided to take his business elsewhere. Tom Weston had seemed like the right choice. "If Kathryn is as good as you say, I want her on my case, too."

"Can't do that, Curt."

"Why the hell not? I'm paying the tab, aren't I?"

Standing, Tom buttoned his suit jacket. "I got the distinct impression Kathryn doesn't want anything to do with you. I'm not going to put one of my employees, particularly a top staff person, in that kind of an awkward position."

"I'm not going to ravish her, man. I just want a chance to get acquainted." Possibly on an intimate level, he admitted, but only to himself.

With an obvious effort to terminate the conversation, Tom walked around to the near side of the desk. "We've got another paralegal who is just as competent to handle any necessary research and do the legwork. I plan to assign him to the case."

"Some friend," Curt groused as he left the office. Kathryn was nowhere to be found. Fortunately the bookkeeper who had received the extra roses was the talkative type.

KATHRYN FILLED her two-cup coffeemaker with the special blend of beans she preferred. It was one of her few extravagances, one she cherished at the end of each long day. After her encounter with Curt and his roses that morning, she decided the coffee would be especially welcome.

Just as she turned on the water tap she heard a knock at the door.

Probably Rudy checking in, she thought, crossing the living room in her stocking feet. As sweet as the man was, Kathryn sensed he was lonely. Once he had mentioned, rather wistfully, that he had left some woman behind when he'd come to Hollywood seeking fame and fortune. Kathryn suspected there were times when Rudy regretted that decision.

To make sure she knew the person on the opposite side of the door, she peered through the peephole.

A headache started at the back of her skull and quickly spread.

Curt Creighton. Looking smug in his leather jacket. Standing outside her apartment door.

For a moment, Kathryn considered pretending not to be at home. But he seemed to be quite aware she was there, his smiling image distorted and magnified through the viewer. As usual, his wavy hair was in slight disarray, the sort of mussiness a woman's fingers itched to comb.

Gritting her teeth, she yanked open the door. "How did you find out where I live?" The need for privacy was why people had unlisted numbers.

"Good evening to you, too, pretty lady." His cheeks creased with that familiar, heart-stopping smile, and the corners of his eyes crinkled. "You're looking charming this evening."

Wearing old slacks and a tatty beige sweater? The man must be blind . . . or think she was the most gullible woman on earth. "I asked how you knew where to find me."

"Oh, we millionaire playboys have our sources." He shrugged noncommittally.

She frowned. "Did Tom give you my address?" If so, her resignation would be on his desk first thing in the morning. There were lots of jobs in town for an experienced paralegal. Her loyalty to Tom's father for giving her a job when she'd been desperate didn't extend into her personal life.

"Not a chance. In fact, he's very protective of you. I gather he thinks I'd lead you to rack and ruin."

Among other destinations, she imagined, not that she'd ever give him the chance. "Then how—"

"That's my little secret. An honorable man never reveals his sources . . . or kisses and tells," he added with a devilish lift of a single eyebrow. "Aren't you going to invite me in?"

"No."

"But I've brought dinner. Since you didn't like the idea of either continental or Mexican, I picked up some Chinese."

He held up a brown paper bag that no doubt contained Louie Garden's equivalent of Family Special number three, egg roll included. In fact, Kathryn caught the scent of soy sauce and spare ribs when he raised the sack. Her stomach growled.

Hungry or not, under no circumstances was she going to eat dinner with Curt Creighton. Certainly not alone with him in her apartment. The guy was too aggressive by far, his constant presence a warm torment that managed to settle low in her body every time he showed up.

And that cocky grin of his! He needed to be put in his place, but good. Did he really think every woman in town would fall all over themselves for one of his sexy smiles? Or because they thought he had a big bank account?

Of course he did, came the irritated response in her head.

But Kathryn wasn't going to add her name to what was no doubt an unending list of his conquests. One run-in with a tabloid photographer was plenty for her.

Eating, however, was a whole different ball game. She hadn't had time to go to the store in days and, except for a frozen vegetarian lasagna, the cupboard was bare.

Lifting her chin to a determined angle, she extended her hands. "Bringing me dinner was very thoughtful. Thank you."

Because Curt had been raised a gentleman, he placed the sack of take-out in Kathryn's hands. Then he watched in shock and growing frustration as the door silently closed in his face.

He blinked, staring at the bronze number 206 on the door for a full thirty seconds before the realization of what had happened finally set in.

"Hey, no. There's enough for both of us." He rapped his knuckles firmly on the door. "Kathryn! That's not fair, you know. You're supposed to invite me in."

Silence was the only response he got.

He knocked again. "Come on, Kathryn," he soothed. "I'm harmless. And I'm hungry." Playing on a woman's sympathy usually worked. "I didn't get any lunch today. My stomach's shrunk clear back to my spine."

Continued silence. Irritating as hell. And downright damaging to a guy's ego. She was sure good at doing a vanishing act when he was around.

The next time he knocked, the door to the apartment across the hall opened and an old guy not much taller than Kathryn peered out at him. "There is something you wanted?" the old guy asked in a phony accent.

Curt glanced at Kathryn's closed door and then at the neighbor. The evening wasn't going the way he'd planned ... a quiet dinner, intimate conversation, maybe a little bit more. Nosy neighbors didn't help.

For now, he figured he'd better chalk up this round to Kathryn. "Naw, I was just leaving." But he'd be back. She could count on it.

As he marched away from the door, a determined smile curled his lips. Courting Kathryn was going to be fun. He couldn't remember the last time he'd been so intrigued with a woman, or felt so challenged. Women like Kathyrn gave a man a reason to get up in the morning.

A few minutes later he'd found a pay phone and dialed the number the bookkeeper had given him. "Cute, pretty lady. Real cute," he said when she answered the phone.

Kathryn's hand squeezed the telephone and her stomach tightened. This guy didn't know when to quit. With a discouraged sigh, she leaned against the kitchen counter where she'd been munching dinner right from the take-out cartons.

"There are laws against stalking a woman," she stated.

"Do you really find me that repulsive?"

Not likely. The opposite was closer to the truth, which was why she didn't want anything to do with Curt. "That's not the point. I'm simply not interested in seeing you socially."

"But a strictly business relationship would be acceptable?"

Kathryn suspected Curt was thinking about *monkey* business, but she didn't say so. "You're one of the firm's clients. If our paths cross in that context, I can see no objection." None she would voice, except to Tom, who would certainly get an earful.

"Good."

She didn't much like the sound of his all-too-easy agreement. He sounded far too pleased with himself.

"So how's the sweet and sour?" he asked.

Stabbing a bite of pork with her fork, she chewed thoughtfully. "Excellent. Very tender. The ribs are delicious, too."

"Glad to hear it."

She pictured him slouched in a phone booth somewhere nearby, maybe even feeling rejected. He probably hadn't had that experience often. She might have even hurt him, she thought with an uncomfortable prick of conscience.

It'd be easy to invite him back to share the meal he'd provided, she rationalized. It would be the kind thing to do. But she didn't dare do that. Not when being around Curt sent her thoughts off in forbidden directions.

"You do understand my position about our... relationship?" she asked. "Strictly business?"

"Sure, pretty lady," he drawled. "Whatever you say."

Liar.

THE FOLLOWING MORNING, Tom came into Kathryn's office almost before she had a chance to tuck her purse away in the filing cabinet. A double row of furrows creased his forehead.

"What's up?" she asked, shrugging off her suit jacket and slipping it onto a padded coat hanger.

"Your office mate called, or rather his wife did. He's got the flu."

"Really? Clarence seemed fine yesterday." Her fellow paralegal was a man in his forties who had attended law school some years ago but had never quite managed to pass the bar exam. His best talents lay in investigative work, which kept him out of the office a lot.

"His wife says he woke up with a nasty cough and a temperature."

"Will I have to cover for him?" That was the usual procedure. If cases were coming up on deadline, everyone pitched in where they were needed. The office staff was good that way, a very cooperative group.

Tom ran one finger around inside his starched, button-down collar, an uncharacteristically self-conscious gesture, as if his shirt were too tight, or he had something troubling on his mind. "We're okay with most of his cases."

"Most?" she asked suspiciously.

"It's the Creighton case . . ."

She stifled a groan. She should have known. She wasn't going to be able to escape that bachelor millionaire.

"We're going to have to file a preliminary response in the next couple of days. I need someone to go out to his place and take a look around to give me a feel for the veracity of the plaintiff's case."

"And the defendant's credibility?" A man to whom perjury would no doubt be a minor offense.

"Curt's okay, Kathryn. Sure, he's had his wild moments. And he does like women, I admit. But I wouldn't ask you to do this if I didn't think you'd be—"

"Safe?" she provided.

"He won't attack you. That's not his style."

No. Seduction was. A technique a lot more difficult to resist than physical force, as far as Kathryn was concerned. "I really don't want to get involved," she said. "Can't you ask someone else?"

"Who? I'd go myself but I'm in court all this week on the Rettorri matter. Lyman and Garcelli are tied up, too. With Clarence out sick, that leaves you." He lowered his voice to his most persuasive tone, the one he used to convince juries to give his clients a break. Nine out of ten times, it worked. "I hate to ask this of you, Kathryn, but we need the Creighton account. It's a big one because the corporation is so visible and has so many interests worldwide. The retainer alone will keep us going so we'll have lots of room in the budget to do our *pro bono* work."

He certainly knew how to push her button. The firm of Weston, Lyman and Garcelli spent a lot of their time helping single mothers get child-support payments, all at no charge. Forcing men to take responsibility for their actions happened to be a cause close to Kathryn's heart.

She blew out a sigh. "All right, Tom, I'll do it. But if Curt tries anything funny...well, the deal's off. You'll have to find some other patsy."

"Understood." She detected a trace of relief in his smile. "He'll be here about ten to take you out to his place."

Her eyes widened. "He's coming here? To pick me up?" Why couldn't she drive herself?

"Yeah. He had some business in town this morning and thought that would be best."

She just bet he did. This whole thing—Clarence suddenly coming down with a mysterious flu, the need for her to visit Curt's Hollywood Hills mansion and the man himself driving her there—smelled of a conspiracy to Kathryn.

Her stomach knotted. She'd very much have to be on her guard.

Chapter Three

She hated being stared at.

Apparently that was not an issue for Curt Creighton. Why else would a man drive a gold Ferrari convertible, a car so sleek and sexy looking it drew the attention of every other driver on the road? Rather like how its owner caught the eye of every passing female. The way his cable-knit sweater tugged across his broad shoulders and the fact that he'd shoved the long sleeves up to reveal muscular forearms were no doubt factors causing the women to gawk.

Then, of course, the smile he generously bestowed on each pedestrian wearing a skirt was enough to raise a woman's morale for days.

Gritting her teeth, Kathryn slid a little deeper into the rich leather upholstery that molded to her body like a soft glove. She supposed she ought to be grateful he hadn't picked her up on his motorcycle.

"You don't look pleased to be assigned to my case." With an expert flick of his wrist, Curt shifted the car and they sped across the intersection when the light turned green.

Kathryn squinted against the bright sunlight, shading her eyes with her hand while at the same time trying to keep flyaway strands of her hair from blowing in her face. "I find it an interesting coincidence that Clarence Middlebury, who should have handled the job, is out sick today."

"My good fortune, I guess."

She frowned. Bribery was a definite possibility, though she hated to think her office mate would be in cahoots with Creighton. "You're taking it well that I conned you out of a Chinese dinner last night."

"Win some, lose some." He slanted her a glance from behind his wraparound dark glasses. "I plan to give you a chance to make it up to me later."

She read that comment as both a threat and a promise. "I'd rather just pay you for the meal." At the moment, she felt a little less clever than when she'd shut the door in his face. This was not a man you should cross, she suspected.

"Oh, I never take money from a lady," he drawled. "Against my principles."

"I'm glad to hear you have some principles," she mumbled under her breath.

Curt's low chuckle let her know he'd heard her nasty comment. "I suspect you've been reading my press clippings. Just because you see something in print doesn't make it true."

"You mean you don't have a half-dozen beauties living on your estate?"

"Well, yeah, that part's true. At least, most of the time."

"And you don't have swinging parties that the police have to break up?"

"Occasionally things get out of hand," he conceded. "But it's not what it seems."

Of course not. The shots she'd seen on the six o'clock news of screaming women running half-clad through the shrubbery were all figments of some cameraman's imagination.

"So you're claiming orgies aren't your style?"

"Absolutely not." He beamed one of his famous smiles in her direction. "Done correctly, a man can only handle one woman at a time."

Somehow she didn't feel in the least relieved by the sincerity in his low, husky voice.

They'd left the busy commercial streets of Century City and West Hollywood behind and were now cruising a winding road that led up into the hills. The car took each turn easily, riding as smoothly as a much larger vehicle but lower to the ground. Though she didn't think they were exceeding the limit, there was a definite sensation of speed. The wind in her face, a man who moved fast sitting behind the wheel, both added to the experience—an experience that produced a fair amount of anxiety somewhere low in Kathryn's belly.

Massive oaks and giant jacarandas lined the street. Huge houses, some three stories high, hid behind hedges and wrought iron fences covered in carefully pruned ivy. From time to time, Kathryn caught a glimpse of immaculately manicured lawns and flower gardens still bright with color, although it was fall.

Forcing herself to relax, she leaned back in the seat and simply enjoyed the view. Shadows cast by tree branches crisscrossed her face. The air smelled fresh, cleansed by the lush growth and removed from the busier, smoggier streets. What a contrast between this neighborhood and her crowded street filled with apartment houses, she mused. No rusting cars with permanently flat tires parked at these curbs.

She smiled to herself. Adjusting to this kind of living would be easy. Not that she'd ever have the chance, unless a private law practice was a lot more lucrative than even she had imagined. But the ambience was definitely seductive.

She shifted her gaze to Curt, eyeing him with newfound suspicion.

Darn it all! This leisurely drive through his exclusive neighborhood was all part of the plan—*his* plan to weaken her defenses.

Well, she'd have none of it. She was here on business, and under duress. Straightening her spine and squaring her shoulders, she resolved not to be lulled again by Curt's subtle and very experienced seductive skills.

The wrought iron gates to the Creighton estate parted the instant before Curt wheeled the car up the curving drive.

Opulent consumption, Kathryn told herself, even as she took in the expanse of beautifully trimmed lawns and elegant, formal flower beds. The antebellum house could have graced a hillside in Georgia before Sherman's march through the state. The scene literally took her breath away.

"I'm glad you like it," Curt said, responding to her audible sigh. He pulled the car to a stop in front of the expansive porch. "I've always thought it was a bit much, but my mother was from the South. Since she was raised in a sharecropper's shack, she figured she deserved this."

"Really?" The end of the word rose on Kathryn's question.

"Yep. She ran away from home at sixteen and worked her way west by waitressing. Finally got herself a modeling job. That's how she met Dad. Wouldn't give him the time of day at first. To hear him tell it, Mom was cussedly independent."

"Good for her."

"The end result was the beginning of Seduction Incorporated. Dad tried everything he could think of to get her into his bed. She'd have none of it."

In spite of herself, Kathryn smiled. "So what finally worked?"

A frown stitched across his forehead. "You know, I don't think either one of my folks ever told us." He shrugged. "Anyway, my mom used to keep a plot of ground out in back where she raised corn and beans and stuff. Claimed it was good to remember her roots, particularly when she made me and my sister help her do the weeding."

The laugh that swept up her throat was irrepressible. "I hope I get to meet your mother."

Curt's hand, warm and slightly rough, palmed her cheek, brushing back her blow-away hair. "I wish you could. But she died in a plane crash when I was ten. I still miss her."

A band tightened around Kathryn's chest in response to his grief. "I'm sorry," she whispered, pressing her cheek more fully into his palm. She rested her hand on his wrist, acutely aware of his strength, the masculine texture of his flesh and the fact that they had shared the same kind of shattering childhood experience.

SUCKERED. Again.

Kathryn stood in the middle of what Curt called the guest bedroom—white carpeted, French Provincial furniture and *scarlet* drapes. She stared down at the large, circular bed, the purported scene of the plaintiff's back injury, then shifted her gaze up to the matching mirror on the ceiling. The scene reflected there left little doubt in her mind. It took no imagination at all to fill in the blanks.

"It's not what it looks like," Curt protested.

"If this case goes to trial, you're dead meat," she told him grimly, "and so is your bank account."

"My dad sort of went back to his old ways after Mom died. He was the one who used this room. Not me."

"I doubt you could get two jurors out of twelve to believe that."

"Well, it's true." He jammed his hands into his pockets. "It's your job to defend me."

Terrific. Maybe she ought to consider a career change.

"I don't know what Tom will say, but my advice is to settle. For any amount she'll agree to."

A muscle rippled at his jaw. "The woman fell out of bed because she was drunk. I wasn't anywhere near her. And I will not pay blood money to any woman just because she thinks I'm an easy mark."

The intensity of Curt's denial startled Kathryn. He'd make a wonderful witness on the stand—sincere, honorable, determined to protect his name. But one picture of this room and he wouldn't have a prayer of winning his case...even if she were both defending him *and* on the jury.

"I suspect it's already too late, but you might want to consider redecorating."

"Yeah. I already talked to my sister about that. She said she'd take care of it." He gave the satin spread a tug to straighten a wrinkle. "Shouldn't we try to re-create the scene, or something?"

Kathryn battled the blush that crept up her neck. "That's not really necessary. Why don't you just tell me what happened?" No way was she going to lie down on that bed while Curt was anywhere nearby. That was one daydream that was better left among her fantasies. "Let's start from the beginning. Was this Roslyn Kellogg just visiting for the night?"

"She'd been living here for about three months."

"I see." Perhaps Curt and his lady friend had had a spat, making Roslyn a scorned woman who wanted to get even by filing the suit.

Curt sat down on the edge of the bed and then stretched out full-length, tucking his hands behind his head on the pillow. He crossed his ankles and smiled up at her in open invitation.

Swallowing hard, Kathryn took a determined step back. "Your shoes will ruin that white satin," she said inanely, trying not to think of how indulgent the fabric would feel brushing against naked flesh.

"I'll be careful."

"Yes, well . . . about Ms. Kellogg . . ."

"She was from Portland, I think. Like a lot of the girls who end up staying here, she blew into town sure she was going to set Hollywood on fire. You know, an acting class or two under her belt and maybe some modeling experience. It rarely works out like they hope. Mostly they run out of money before they can get themselves established. Then their choices are really limited."

"Are you trying to tell me you run a shelter for unemployed models and wannabe starlets?"

"Sort of. Lucy—that's my sister—is in the casting part of the business. When she sees a gal in trouble, and assuming she's a decent enough kid, Sis sometimes invites her home. We've got plenty of extra rooms."

"And you're here to chaperon the young ladies who are down on their luck."

His cocky grin creased both cheeks. "I admit it's a tough job, but somebody has to do it."

Pursing her lips, Kathryn fought the responding smile that threatened. The man was impossible. And irresistibly charming.

In an amazingly agile move, Curt was on his feet and standing very close to her. "You can do it. Go ahead," he urged.

"Do what?" Reaching out to touch one of his tempting, elongated dimples came to mind, but she didn't dare do that.

"Smile. You did once in the car—I saw you. You even laughed a little. Now I want to really see you let one loose."

"Curt..." she protested, "we're supposed to be discussing business." Noting the persistent twinkle in his blue-green eyes, along with the length of his lashes and the well-formed arch of his eyebrows, wasn't on Kathryn's agenda. At least, such details shouldn't have been. But they were, along with the acute awareness of his spicy after-shave and his overpowering masculinity.

"That doesn't mean we can't have a little fun." He ran the back of his knuckles slowly down her cheek to her jaw, then brushed his thumb across her lower lip. "Just a little smile. For starters."

As a responding heat curled through Kathryn's body, the voice of her conscience tartly asked where that smile might lead. The answer was all too obvious—to the middle of a king-size, circular bed.

Run, the voice warned, run as fast as you can.

Demonstrating considerable self-restraint, she firmly grasped Curt's wrist and moved his hand away from her face. "Now then, Mr. Creighton, why don't you tell me exactly what happened the night in question."

Curt let his hand fall to his side. This lady was one tough cookie. His usual moves weren't working at all. Maybe he was simply out of practice. Extended celibacy had a way of making a guy rusty, he supposed.

"One of the other gals had a birthday that night," he explained. "Somebody had brought in a few bottles of bubbly and we all celebrated."

"You included?"

"I had a glass or two, I admit. But I had a trip scheduled to New York the next day so I hit the sack early."

Her gaze darted suspiciously to the bed. "Your other . . . houseguests could confirm that?"

"Probably. Assuming they were sober enough to remember."

The grim set of her pouty lips suggested she didn't believe him.

"I was in my own bedroom, sound asleep, *alone*," he emphasized, "when I heard Roz scream."

"And where is your bedroom located?"

With a flick of his head, he gestured toward the connecting double doors.

"How convenient. Do you mind if I look?"

"Not at all." His temper rising, Curt marched across the room, opened the door and motioned her inside. The lady wasn't giving him an inch. No woman could be that much of an ice maiden. Or be such a Doubting Thomasina. Unless she'd been hurt by some guy, he realized with a flash of insight. That would account for her effort to be so aloof even when he could detect her pulse racing at that delicate spot on the column of her slender neck. A spot he had an incredible urge to kiss.

Yes, that was the problem, he decided, smiling smugly to himself as she stepped into his bedroom. All it would take was a bit of time, gentle handling and a fair dose of patience. Then Ms. Katie Prim would be visiting his bedroom with more than a lawsuit on her mind.

Once across the threshold, Kathryn drew in a quick breath, filling her lungs with the combined scent of rich leather and polished wood. A man's room. Heavy, masculine furniture rested on a lush carpet of deep green, as though she'd just stepped into a forest glade. Exterior latticework shaded a wall of windows, muting the colors in the room, while still allowing an unobstructed view of the city. At night she suspected the lights would be like a magic carpet of twinkling diamonds. Intoxicating. Romantic.

Fighting the mesmerizing image, Kathryn shifted her attention back to the room.

On the remaining three walls, an array of black-and-white photos were individually spotlighted. Each of the subjects was a study in depth depicted in an instant of time—two youngsters giddy with excitement as they raced into the ocean; a pair of teenagers tentatively experiencing what looked like their first kiss; the heartbreak of a wizened woman digging through a garbage can for something to eat. Kathryn's gaze was drawn again and again to the photo of a mother nursing her infant, the splay of the child's tiny hand soft against her breast, the look of love in the woman's eyes a palpable thing that reached well beyond a single dimension into the space that surrounded her. Emotion tightened in Kathryn's chest and thickened in her throat. If only...

"Who...who's the photographer?" she asked, breaking the silence in the room.

"I am. Before Dad died that's how I spent my time. Taking pictures. Not that he particularly approved. Now..." A resigned shrug completed the sentence for him.

"You're very talented." Could a man who captured that much emotion on film be as superficial as the tabloids reported? she wondered. Or would he have to have his own depth of character in order to see it so clearly in others?

Her gaze slid to his bed. With a guilty rush of heat to her cheeks, she realized she'd be much more easily tempted to make love with Curt in this room than in the adjacent one. A thought she squelched almost as quickly as it occurred.

She cleared her throat. "So you were asleep here when Ms. Kellogg fell out of bed?" Asleep in the buff, she mentally added, trying valiantly to block that image, too.

The predatory glint in his eyes suggested he knew what she'd been thinking. "That's what I've been telling you."

"If any of your other houseguests are around who were here that night, I'd like to talk with them."

"You got it, pretty lady. Their schedules are kinda irregular, what with casting calls and auditions, but they'll probably be back by the time we finish lunch."

"Lunch?" she echoed. At no time during Kathryn's conversation with Tom Weston had he mentioned anything about her having a meal with Curt.

"Sure. Marvin's setting it up for us around the pool."

"I don't really have time—"

"Of course you do." Slipping his arm around her waist in an easy, proprietary way, he escorted her out the sliding-glass door. "I squared it with Tom before we left the office. Said we'd probably be gone most of the day."

"You're pushy, Creighton. Really pushy."

"They tell me it comes from being raised with too much wealth." Gently but firmly, he propelled her down the slate steps of the terraced yard until they reached the pool level. The expanse of crystal clear water sparkled like a turquoise heart suspended somewhere between the bright sky and the hazy city below, a magical place designed to bewitch the innocent.

Fortunately Kathryn counted herself among those not easily lured into forbidden territory. At least, that was no longer the case.

If she had expected Marvin to be an English-style butler she would have been all wrong. With a pockmarked face, drooping eyelids, a zigzag nose and meaty hands, he looked more like a well-mannered boxer long past his prime. In fact, she doubted he'd ever had much success in the ring to end up looking like that.

Still, the shrimp salad he served was delicately flavored with a touch of sherry in the dressing, and the croissants were buttery rich. Kathryn was finally beginning to relax and enjoy the meal—and Curt's company, she admitted a bit warily—when the inquisition began.

"So tell me about this hometown of yours," Curt asked, his brilliant eyes gazing at her intently over the top of his glass of white wine. "In central California, you said?"

"Waverly," she responded, not eager to discuss her past.

He acknowledged her brief reply with a thoughtful nod. "I think I own an interest in a raisin farm up that way."

"You don't know?"

He shrugged, which she took to mean that he had so many investments it was hard to keep track. "So what is Waverly like?" he asked, returning to his original question.

"A typical small town, I suppose." Filled with small, narrow-minded people—replicas of her father—all of whom had made Kathryn feel like a Jezebel.

"So why'd you leave?"

With an easy lift of her shoulders, she provided the answer most people accepted without question. "I like the excitement of a big city."

Frowning skeptically, he leaned forward, placing his wineglass next to his plate with considerable precision. Sunlight caught the light covering of hair on his muscular forearm, tinting the soft swirls with red and brown. "You like excitement?" he questioned in a low, suggestive voice.

"Well, maybe excitement was a poor choice of words," she corrected, fiddling with the stem of her own wineglass. "The city is a place where you can remain anonymous. People leave you alone. I like that."

"I see. You came to L.A. not because you like concerts, or art galleries, or swinging-singles clubs. You came to L.A. so you could hide out." He covered her hand with his in what could have been construed as a sympathetic gesture...or one that was far too intimate.

She concluded it was the latter. "I didn't say that. I prefer living in a city because—" She tried to pull her hand away.

He didn't relinquish his grip. "Because you can meet guys like me."

She sputtered. His teasing grin was about as wide as the Grand Canyon. That line was so bad it wouldn't have worked on a fifteen-year-old girl right off the Greyhound bus. She knew it, and she could tell he did, too. And in spite of all that, or maybe because of it, Kathryn laughed...out loud. The happy sound was unfamiliar, and she felt facial muscles pull in a way she hadn't felt in a long time. Good grief, what had she been missing?

His responding smile sent a warm burst of longing right to her heart. "Gotcha," he said, squeezing her hand.

As she shook her head in amused disbelief, from the corner of her eye Kathryn caught movement at the far end of the pool.

The two long-legged strangers didn't simply walk toward the poolside table where Curt and Kathryn sat beneath a yellow-and-white umbrella, rather they fairly flew at them with effervescent enthusiasm, their spiked heels clicking a staccato beat across the decking. Wearing matching miniscule skirts—designed for ten-year-olds, Kathryn thought unkindly—they were the sexiest pair of blondes she had ever seen in real life.

Kathryn stifled a surprising surge of female competitiveness. It wasn't as if she had a personal interest in Curt Creighton, she reminded herself. But if she did, you could bet your last dollar these two gals would be asked to turn in their front-door keys in a hurry.

"We did it, Curt, honey!" one woman cried.

Curt's fork froze in midair. Talk about lousy timing. Ms. Prim-and-Proper was finally beginning to unbend a little. Her smile was terrific; her laugh a low, sultry sound that made him think of warm chocolate drizzled over a sundae. *Sweet, so sweet.*

Now LaVerne and LaVilla, the Radisson twins, had shown up to break the mood.

He stood. Before he could say a word, LaVerne—or maybe it was LaVilla—had wrapped her arms around his neck.

"We got the part! A commercial! Both of us! Isn't that, like, wild?"

He groaned. "Terrific, girls. I'm happy for you both." Maybe they'd earn enough money to move out on their own. The other twin—LaVilla, he thought—planted a juicy kiss on his cheek.

"We had to, like, come tell you right away. And thank you, thank you, thank you."

As he was being peppered with kisses from both sides, Curt caught a glimpse of Kathryn. This was not the impression he had intended to make. Her expression was so grim, he expected to see smoke coming out her ears at any moment.

"Look, ladies, I'm glad you got the part. Really I am." He tried to extricate himself from their enthusiastic embrace. It was like untangling from a bout with an octopus. "But there's somebody here you need to talk to."

With their arms still draped around various parts of his anatomy, the pair glanced toward Kathryn and spoke almost in unison.

"Well, hi, honey."

"You gonna move in with Curt, too?"

Kathryn lifted her suddenly very tense chin. "Certainly not." Standing, she gave him a look that practically made him bleed. "Mr. Creighton, if you'll provide Mr. Weston with a list of your *friends*—" she paused, letting the icy emphasis she'd placed on the last word sink in "—who witnessed the incident, someone from the office will contact them as soon as possible."

"Now don't go lettin' us scare you off, honey," one of the twins insisted. "You know what our little Curt-baby always says. The more the merrier." Her giggle resembled the sound of a file being scraped vigorously across metal.

Kathryn raised her eyebrows. *"Curt-baby?"* She didn't know what was wrong with her. A sense of panic surged through her midsection and her palms had gone all clammy. It wasn't that Curt's relationship with these twins mattered to her on a personal level. Not even close, she assured herself. But their suggestion, their mere implication, that she would even consider moving in with a man, had sent her defense mechanisms into high gear.

An hysterical need to get away assaulted her reason. She'd likely have to explain herself to her employer later, for failing to thoroughly investigate their client's case, but for now she simply couldn't help herself. Her father's accusing voice rang too loudly in her ears, even after all these years.

Managing to get himself free of the twins, Curt chased Kathryn halfway across the patio. "Both LaVerne and LaVilla were here that night. They can tell you—"

"I'm very sorry, Mr. Creighton," she said, marching across the flagstones like a soldier on a mission. "But I've just remembered I have an appointment this afternoon. If you'll please ask Marvin to call me a cab."

He folded his fingers around her upper arm and felt the tension radiating from her. "I'll take you back to your office."

"I much prefer a taxi."

"This isn't what you think," he said under his breath.

"And what is that, Mr. Creighton? That perhaps I don't approve of men having harems? How very old-fashioned of me."

"Some guy really burned you, didn't he?" he said in a soft whisper. "That's why you're so damned uptight."

The color drained from her face. Even her smattering of freckles seemed to fade. "My personal life is no concern of yours. Now let…me…go." She bit off each word for emphasis.

With no other choice, Curt released her. He watched as she continued her march toward the house, her shoulders square, her spine straight as an arrow. The woman was hurting and he didn't know why.

"Damn," he muttered, vaguely aware the twins were helping themselves to the uneaten desserts on the table.

Somebody had to show Kathryn not all guys were schmucks. He, Curt Creighton, bachelor millionaire, was the ideal candidate for the job.

Chapter Four

"There is a man outside, *mon amie*," Rudy warned the next morning. "The one who was here before."

As she let her neighbor into her apartment, Kathryn popped the last bite of toast into her mouth and gulped down her coffee. "Who are you talking about?"

"He is very big, this man, and, yes, I think he is handsome." The slight lift of his shoulders communicated his indifference to such matters. "But he is dangerous, I believe."

Creighton. God, his multiple phone calls last night should have convinced her he wouldn't let her off the hook with an impersonal taxi ride home. Not that she'd picked up the phone for any of his calls. But her answering machine had almost run out of tape.

Persistent devil.

If her boss hadn't told her Curt was harmless, she might have been frightened by his determination. Instead, her biggest fear was her own reaction, the unfamiliar—unwelcome—sense of pleasure that came with knowing he was loitering outside her door.

"What does he want from me?" she protested with a low groan, trying to deny both the man's presence and her own feelings.

"I do not know, *chérie,* but if you wish to avoid him I believe I have a plan."

"Anything to avoid Curt Creighton. What do you have in mind?"

"Ah." He grinned in satisfaction. "You and I are about the same size, no?"

"I suppose..."

"Then you must loan me a dress, a pair of your high heels and the keys to your car." He handed her a worn leather key case. His dark eyes twinkled with mischief. "We will exchange vehicles, no? I will leave first, this scoundrel who waits in the shrubbery will follow and you will be able to escape in my car."

"But you can't masquerade as a woman." In spite of Rudy's size, he was very masculine in the way he walked and held himself, rather like a bantam rooster.

He flicked his wrist in an effeminate gesture and swiveled his hips.

Kathryn choked on her coffee. It seemed her neighbor had unlimited acting talents for both voice and mannerisms.

"Once again you forget I am an actor," Rudy insisted. "No role is beyond me, even that of a woman. I have observed your movements for some time. To copy them is ever so simple, my dear. I will have the man eating out of my hand, no?''

"Well...if you're sure." Kathryn really didn't want to deal with Curt face-to-face. Her feelings about him were very much at odds with what her sensible mind kept echoing. One minute she was recalling the way his eyes crinkled with amusement and she found herself wishing she could see his smile again, and the next minute she was fighting a surge of panic that threatened to disable her with its intensity. The sensation was disconcerting and thoroughly unexpected. No man had ever affected her in quite that same way.

She dug into her purse and pulled out her car keys. "The clutch is a little touchy," she warned.

"Not to worry. I will master the machinery as I do a new role."

Somewhat doubtful Curt would be fooled, she found a dress she thought would fit Rudy and an old pair of heels that had seen better days. He selected a sweater from her wardrobe, then assured her that a scarf over his head would complete the disguise.

A few minutes later, she watched out the window as Rudy raced toward her car, hopped in behind the steering wheel and roared off down the street. Hot on his trail came Curt in his Ferrari.

She chortled softly to herself. "Round two, Mr. Creighton. Gotcha again!"

WITHIN SIX BLOCKS, suspicion began to gnaw at Curt's awareness. Another half mile and he was sure he'd been conned.

Kathryn, or rather her car, was heading in the opposite direction from her office. Though it was possible she had an early-morning appointment elsewhere, the random turns suggested a scenic tour rather than a direct route from point A to point B.

His jaw clenched.

Kathryn Prim was the most elusive woman he'd ever met.

Accelerating, he pulled up beside the VW Rabbit, then cut the driver off at the next signal. He jumped out of his car and ran back to find out what was going on.

Reality slammed him in the gut.

The wrinkled old guy peeking coyly back at him from beneath a brightly colored scarf was definitely not Kathryn.

"There was something you wanted, young man?" the impostor taunted, fluttering his eyelashes. "Such an impetuous boy."

Curt hammered the heel of his hand against the edge of the car roof. Her neighbor! How could he have mistaken the old man for Kathryn?

It wouldn't happen again, he vowed. Not in this lifetime. She could play this cat-and-mouse game all she liked. Eventually he would be the one who pounced.

KATHRYN FORCED HERSELF to concentrate on her work. With Rudy's help, she'd successfully avoided Curt's pursuit that morning. But she had the uncomfortable feeling that sooner or later another shoe would drop. Her current assignment, researching case law on condo conversions, definitely wasn't holding her attention.

Her gaze slid from the law book to the phone. She ought to call her sister, Alice, to arrange a time and place to get together, though given her work and school schedules Kathryn knew that wouldn't be easy. At least at this time of day she could be sure her father wouldn't be home to answer the phone.

At the sound of whispers behind her, Kathryn turned toward the open door of her office. Her eyes widened.

"Miss Prim?" The young man standing in her doorway wore a costume that vaguely made him look like one of Robin Hood's merry men, green tights and pointed hat included. A mandolin hung from a strap around his neck. "Special delivery, ma'am." Smiling, he strummed a musical chord.

Feeling her stomach knot, she realized the other shoe had dropped like an anvil.

Kathryn had heard of singing telegrams but never anything quite as extravagant as this. No doubt Seduction Incorporated had tenors on call all across the country, balladeers carefully rehearsed to sing romantic songs at the drop of a charge-card number.

She cringed inwardly at the dreadful, individualized lyrics. "My love has been gath...ern for my beautiful Kath...ryn." She wished she could slide under her desk and escape the curious looks of her fellow employees who hovered around the door to her office. Forcing herself to sit erect and expressionless, with as much dignity as she could muster under the circumstances, she fought the angry heat that flushed her cheeks. Her stomach churned. Curt Creighton was going to hear from her, all right— loud and clear. He had no right to interrupt her work and disrupt her life. He was damaging her reputation. She'd have none of it. She'd worked far too hard to develop an image she could be proud of. He wasn't going to blow it all for her now.

When the young tenor began the third verse, she called a halt to the concert.

"Thank you very much," she said firmly. "That will be quite sufficient."

He stopped in mid-phrase. "But I'm getting paid to sing six verses, ma'am. I've got them all memorized. Don't you want to hear the rest?"

"No." She stood, took his shoulders and turned him like a recalcitrant child toward the door. "It will be our little secret that you only got through two of them before I threw you out on your ear. Or called the cops," she warned. "Your choice."

"Well, sure, lady, I'll go. But you gotta take the candy." From a carryall bag slung over his shoulder he retrieved a giant, heart-shaped box. Five pounds if it was an ounce.

"I don't *want* the candy."

"Ah, come on, Kathryn," argued a smiling secretary who had her eye on the way the minstrel's legs were snugged into skin-hugging tights. "Be a good sport."

She stifled a groan. "The candy's yours, Julia." The guy, too, if that's what she wanted. "Be my guest."

Amid much shuffling for position, the singer went off down the hall with a clutch of giggling women surrounding him. Only Marcy Higgins, the aging bookkeeper, remained outside Kathryn's door, gazing longingly after those who had left.

"That Mr. Creighton is the most romantic man in the world," Marcy said with a sigh. "First roses, and now candy delivered by a minstrel. And Mr. Creighton is so handsome, too. If only my husband wasn't such a couch potato." She sighed again, her wrinkled face dissolving into a wistful expression.

"Yes, well..." At the rate he was going, Curt would have the entire female staff of Weston, Lyman and Garcelli turned into his own personal fan club. Except for Kathryn. Somehow she'd have to put a stop to his antics. As soon as possible. "Do you by chance have Mr. Creighton's phone number?" she asked Marcy.

"Of course, dear. I know you want to thank him. Such a sweet man." She smiled coyly, as if Curt could do no wrong. "I'll just find the number for you in my files."

Fuming, Kathryn followed Marcy to her cubicle. *Thanking* Curt wasn't exactly what she had in mind. Threatening him with a restraining order was closer to the truth.

"By the way," she said as she accepted the piece of paper with Curt's number scribbled on it, "I made a phone call to Waverly, California, the other evening. To my sister. When the bill comes, let me know how much it is and I'll write you a check."

"I'll make a note," Marcy agreed.

With a resolute set to her jaw, Kathryn returned to her office, closed the door for privacy and sat down at her desk. She dialed Curt's number.

He answered on the first ring.

For a moment, the familiar sound of his voice caused Kathryn's throat to tighten with unexpected emotion. Even a simple hello from Curt Creighton had a seductive power over Kathryn, but she was determined to fight it.

"Your candy delivery disrupted the entire office this morning," she said abruptly.

"You're welcome," he replied with a self-confident grin in his voice.

"I'm going to bill you for the time lost."

"No problem."

It wouldn't be for a millionaire, she realized. Her hourly charges were penny-ante stuff, pocket change for a guy like Creighton. "If you persist in this continued harassment, I'm going to get a restraining order.''

''If you hadn't ducked out on me this morning, I would have given you the candy in person,'' he reminded her reasonably. ''Then I wouldn't have had to upset your office routine. You would have thanked me kindly, and I would have asked you out. Just like I was trying to do on the phone last night. How does this evening sound? About seven, for dinner?''

''I have night class. Besides, I don't—''

''Tomorrow night, then.''

''No.'' The man was the most thickheaded, stubborn...

''Let's see...'' He paused thoughtfully. ''I know this rock group. Three or four guys. Big amplifiers. Guitars. Base fiddle. A great beat and they're always looking for an extra gig. I suppose they could deliver—''

''You wouldn't.''

''That'd probably get the attention of everybody in the building. We could start 'em playing as they come up in the elevator. By the time they get to your floor, the whole place ought to be rockin'.''

She felt the hot press of tears at the back of her eyes. ''Please, Curt...'' Her voice caught on a sob. ''Don't you understand? You embarrassed me. In front of my friends. The people I have to work with every day. What must they think of me?'' And what must they be saying behind her back. Those giggles she'd heard hadn't been entirely because of the singer's cute buns, she was sure.

Her plea managed to silence him.

She circled her temple with her fingertips waiting for his reply. She pressed her lips tightly together. Surely now he'd agree to leave her alone.

"You're right," he said in a husky voice. "I apologize."

She closed her eyes and exhaled a relieved sigh. "Then you understand I don't want any more gifts from you? Nor do I want you to call me either here or at home."

"No more presents? Not even one tiny little—"

"No."

"Tell you what, pretty lady. I promise I won't embarrass you anymore. How's that?"

She gritted her teeth. "Not good enough, Creighton."

"Then my efforts to seduce you are failing miserably? You're not even the least bit tempted?"

Her damn sense of honesty caused her to hesitate a beat too long. "I'm not going to admit to anything that might incriminate me." Except those very words spoke volumes about his effective seduction techniques. *Incriminate, hell, she'd just damned herself!*

The sound of his warm laughter reached out like a teasing caress. He'd heard the none-too-subtle nuances in her voice, the vacillation she'd tried to hide. The guy wasn't going to quit. Not with the opening she'd provided. Kathryn knew she was helpless to halt his determined onslaught on her defenses. At some very deep level, one she was afraid to acknowledge, she wasn't entirely sure she wanted him to stop.

THE FOLLOWING MORNING a discreet package wrapped in brown paper and marked Personal arrived on her desk. With equal parts curiosity and anxiety, she slipped off the wrapper. No card. No return address. But it didn't take a genius to guess the sender.

The silk scarf slid sinuously from the box, the fabric flowing across her fingers like a soft rush of warm water. Kathryn lifted the fabric to her cheek. The gentle caress stroked her flesh like the touch of a lover.

Her heart lunged against her ribs as she imagined Curt selecting the scarf, palming it in his broad hands and folding it carefully into the slender box. Had he envisioned the length of his gift gently encircling the column of her neck? she wondered. Or draped across her hair?

Dear God, she shouldn't be thinking about things like that—images that made her contemplate temptations she didn't dare consider. As a teenager she'd been foolish. She'd vowed not to repeat that behavior.

The sound of Tom Weston's voice jolted her out of her reverie. "Have you got the file on the Ikazawa tax case?" he asked from the doorway.

"Yes." The word scraped up her constricted throat. Hurriedly she stuffed the scarf back into the box and shoved it into her top desk drawer. She'd send the gift back to Curt. She simply wouldn't let him tempt her that way. "I'll bring it right in."

"Whenever you have a chance. I've got to see Garcelli about another matter first."

THE DAY AFTER THAT a gold butterfly stickpin arrived, again in an unmarked box. The next day it was a slender book of poems, each verse speaking eloquently of romance. Thumbing through the pages, Kathryn sighed, fighting the smile that trembled at the corners of her lips. The man was determined to drive her crazy.

By the end of the week, the simple arrival of the mail clerk in her office brought a tightness to Kathryn's chest, and a warm rush of wanting much lower in her body. Though she hadn't spoken a word to Curt Creighton since the incident with the candy delivery, it was clear the man was a master of seduction.

The fact that she had dutifully—regretfully, she admitted with a wry twist of her lips—rewrapped each present and mailed it back to him hadn't slowed Curt down a bit.

After work she eagerly headed for the gym and her jazzercise class. A good workout would keep her mind off the man.

Dressed in her leotards and ratty leg warmers, she entered the mirrored room, glancing around to see if she recognized anyone.

Her heart lodged in her throat.

Across the room she spotted Curt...waiting for her.

His cocky gaze was an indecent assault on her senses. He gave her a slow, satisfied perusal, a look that raised Kathryn's temperature by several degrees. Every exposed inch of her skin flushed, along with a fair amount of her flesh duly hidden beneath form-revealing, stretchy fabric. He didn't try to disguise his intentions. The glint in his eye was there for anyone to see. It said he was willing to play any game she chose, but eventually she'd lose...or surrender. Whichever came first, he'd be around to collect the prize. Her.

Wearing shorts, he sauntered toward her in an easy, athletic stroll. His bare legs looked tanned and muscular with a fine roughening of cinnamon brown hair. A faded T-shirt that used to be blue tugged across his broad chest. Kathryn thought that with his brawny arms Curt would look more at home in a weight lifting room, rather than in a dance class.

"So how's your week been?" he asked with a casual air of interest.

"Busy." The word nearly stuck in her throat. "How did you know where to find me?"

He shrugged. "Coincidence. Pure coincidence that I decided to do a little aerobics and just happened to pick the same gym where you're a member."

"Right. Like Mr. Booth just happened to be at the Ford Theater the same night Lincoln had tickets? Do you have spies everywhere?"

"Are you suggesting I'm in such good shape I don't need a little exercise?" His grin was a masterful combination of amusement and male ego.

She studied him critically, letting her gaze rove over him in much the same way he had looked at her. "I suppose some women like men with little 'love handles,'" she suggested straight-faced, knowing from the way his shirt fit that his stomach was rock hard—all muscle with little extra fat.

"I don't..." he sputtered. Frowning, he felt around his waist. "Do I?"

"You do know this is an advanced class, don't you?" she warned. "The instructor gives a real cardiac and lung workout. Most beginners prefer—"

"I can handle it. I'm in pretty good shape."

He was such a hunk, half the women in the class had already given him the once-over...and been duly impressed. So was Kathryn, but she wasn't about to give away that little secret. Or let on that at the first sight of him she'd experienced the forbidden thrill of excitement. "I wouldn't want you to damage yourself by overdoing. Strained muscles are a frequent

injury for someone who isn't in top-notch condition, or who tries to do too much too soon. Cardiac
arrest is possible, too. Particularly for a mature man.
That is a little gray I see at your temples, isn't it?''
Just a touch that made him look distinguished rather
than totally boyish.

His frown turned into a scowl. "I'll manage." A
muscle rippled at his jaw. "I'm not exactly over the
hill, you know."

"Of course not." With that, she pirouetted away,
taking her place near the front of the class as the energetic instructor called them to order. She hid her
smug smile.

"Well, hell..." Curt muttered. He found a spot
where he could keep an eye on Kathryn and tried to
follow the directions of the pixielike instructor. He
ran his hand across his sideburns. He wasn't *that*
gray, was he?

The stretching part went reasonably well. Maybe
he wasn't as flexible as all these lithe women were—
Kathryn included—but he could at least keep up. The
few guys in the room weren't all that agile, either.
And they were wimps, he thought with satisfaction.

One, two, three... he grunted as he bent to touch
his toes. Kathryn had a great tush, he noted. Four,
five, six... he raised his arms as directed, liking the
feminine curve of her back, the soft slope of her
shoulders. As she swayed from side to side, the out-
line of her ribs visible, he wished he could circle her
waist with his hands. She had her hair tied back in a

ponytail that shifted with each movement. The effect was hypnotic...enticing.

He began to breathe a little harder as the rhythm picked up.

Kathryn, he noticed, had hardly broken a sweat yet, while he could already feel a trickle of moisture edging down his face. The muscles in his calves yelped with the unfamiliar strain. Maybe women were made differently than guys in more ways than the most obvious.

The music seemed louder and faster. He struggled to keep up.

His lungs burned; his arms felt as if they'd been injected with a ton of lead. His legs weren't doing much better.

With the tail of his shirt, he wiped the stinging sweat from his eyes. How the hell had he gotten himself into this mess?

But he sure wasn't going to quit. Not a chance; not with Kathryn cruising along in what looked like overdrive.

The woman was too damned perfect! *Everyone* ought to sweat.

He stumbled and some gal caught him before he could make a fool of himself by falling on his face.

"Maybe you ought to rest a minute," she suggested in dulcet tones.

"I'm okay," he said between gasping breaths. Actually, he was probably out of his mind and just didn't know it yet. Maybe next time he would think twice before bribing Tom Weston's bookkeeper with a box of chocolates to find out where Kathryn went after work.

His lips pulled back into a forced grin when the workout finally ended. Not for a minute would he let his classmates know the next breath he drew was likely to be his last.

Trying not to stagger, he made his way to the side of the room, leaned back against the mirror and felt his knees give out. He slowly slid to the floor. Blackness threatened.

"Are you okay?"

Kathryn's voice was sweet and concerned, like the feel of rose petals skimming across his aching body. If he'd had the strength, he would have reached out to touch her, perhaps caress her soft cheek with his fingertips, or brush back damp tendrils of hair that softened the oval of her face. But his arms appeared to have become disengaged from his body. At least, they were unresponsive to his simple commands. His focus seemed a bit off kilter, too, since he seemed to see Kathryn actually smiling at him. She had great teeth—white and even. Maybe the whole excruciating experience had been worth the effort, he mused.

"Pretty lady..."

She used a towel to wipe the sweat from his face. He liked a nurturing woman. Then from somewhere she produced a container of water. He drank eagerly.

"Not too fast," she warned.

He coughed and sputtered. "It was probably too hot in here for all this exercise. They oughta turn up the air-conditioning with so many people."

"You're right." With her hand, Kathryn brushed a lock of his damp hair back from his forehead. The man was crazy. He could have really hurt himself, overexerting like he had. Though he was in good physical shape, aerobics required more than solid muscle. "Rest a minute and you'll feel much better."

"I'll be able to go another round or two in a minute."

"Sure." Perspiration darkened his shirt in a wide V. She doubted he had an ounce of energy left. But she certainly wouldn't call him a quitter. "Truth is, I'm worn to a frazzle," she said, offering him an opportunity to save face. "I need to cool down and take a shower. How 'bout you?"

He raised a lecherous eyebrow. "If that's an invitation to join you, I'd be happy to accept."

"Not a chance, fella."

"Okay. Let's consider an alternative. I've wiped myself out enjoying your fun and games, and pretty much made a fool out of myself in the process. It's only fair you give me a chance to redeem my good name."

She gazed at him suspiciously. "What do you mean by that?"

"I'm a hell of a lot better on the tennis court than I am at aerobics. How 'bout a match. Tomorrow. My place."

"No, thanks." She stood and backed away. His Hollywood Hills home was definitely a dangerous place for a woman to visit alone.

He struggled to his feet, leaving a damp sweat mark on the mirror where he had leaned back. "Where's your sense of justice?"

"It has nothing to do with—"

"Then I'll make a bargain with you. I'll play you left-handed. You beat me two out of three sets and I'm gone. History. I won't darken your door again. I promise."

"That's ridiculous. I may not be a spectacular tennis player, but you can't beat me if you play with the wrong hand. That's a terrible bet."

"Then we're on for tomorrow?"

The niggling voice of reason warned Kathryn she was being conned. But how? "You're willing to stop harassing me if I beat you at tennis?"

"That's the deal. And in return, if by some miracle I win, you agree to go out with me."

She scowled.

"Once. That's all we're talking about. One little innocent date. What could it hurt?"

She mentally humphed. Nothing about Creighton was innocent. Even so, she was sorely tempted to take the bet. She had little to lose, she rationalized. And to be rid of Curt once and for all might be worth an afternoon of her time. That didn't, however, mean she was willing to take him at his word.

"Tell you what, Creighton. I'll accept your challenge but with one condition."

"What's that?"

"That we play mixed doubles. And I get to bring my own partner."

Curt's forehead stitched into a frown. "That's not exactly what I had in mind."

"I know," she said brightly. That was precisely why she was going to ask a very good client of the firm to come along tomorrow.

Chapter Five

"Played at Wimbledon, eh?" Curt eyed the graying tennis player. As trim and fit as a man twenty years his junior, the old pro definitely wasn't over the hill yet.

"Stefan was seeded in the top twelve professional tennis players for nearly ten years," Kathryn said a bit too smugly, "and won men's doubles twice at Wimbledon."

"Three times," Stefan corrected with an easy smile.

That news did not please Curt. He should have known Kathryn would try to outmaneuver him, this time with a devilishly good-looking silver fox. "Yeah, well, I asked LaVerne and LaVilla to be my partner."

"One at a time, I trust," Kathryn said sharply.

Amused at her tone, Curt lifted a mocking eyebrow. "That's how I've always preferred my women," he reminded her.

Color stained her cheeks and she made a low, exasperated sound deep in her throat. Damn, she looked good in shorts. Nice legs, lightly tanned, calves that were made for a man to palm and well-turned ankles.

She wore a sun visor that shaded the freckles that kissed her nose. Her hair pulled back into a ponytail took on the color of sunlight shot through with threads of fire. Curt itched to feel the weight of the silken strands wrapped around his fingers.

"Can we get this over with?" she urged.

Curt signaled the twins to join them.

As the two long-legged young women promenaded across the tennis court, Curt noted Stefan's interested appraisal. The silver fox still had a youthful eye for the ladies. Perhaps Curt could put that understandable human frailty to appropriate use.

"Mr. Lunada," the twins crooned in unison following Curt's introduction. "What an honor to meet you."

"Could we get your autograph?" one asked.

"Our little brother back home would be thrilled. He plays on the high school tennis team, you know."

"Varsity."

"Of course, the school isn't all that big."

"My dears…" Stefan generously bestowed a light kiss on each young woman's cheek. "It is *you* who honor this old man with your charming presence."

The twins giggled.

Kathryn rolled her eyes.

Smiling, Curt came up with a plan.

In the first two minutes of warm-up shots, it was obvious that Curt and LaVerne—or LaVilla—were outclassed on the court. Stefan had a hundred-mile-an-hour forehand and a backhand that sliced the ball in half. Curt didn't even want to consider the old pro's serve, a speeding bullet that threatened to blast a hole right through the strings of his very expensive racquet, assuming he could manage to get his racquet somewhere in the vicinity of the ball.

Kathryn was pretty darn good, too, fully a match for either of the twins. For Curt, as well, if he was honest with himself. He and Kathryn would make a pretty good team. Not that she seemed eager to consider that possibility.

But neither of his opponents worried Curt. He had an unbeatable secret weapon—two of them.

Taking a break, his breath sawing through his lungs more than he liked and sweat dripping down his face, Curt huddled with his partners at the baseline. Both ladies enthusiastically gave their support to his plan.

Curt strolled with casual ease to the net, picked up a couple of balls he hadn't been able to return and lured Stefan within whispering distance.

"I could use your help, old buddy," Curt said.

"A few pointers on your backhand?" Stefan asked.

"Not exactly. You see, winning this tennis match is my last chance to get a date with Kathryn."

"Yes. So she informs me. All we need do is beat you in two games, a feat that should not be difficult, and then—"

"I'd like to arrange a trade."

Stefan looked at him curiously. "A trade?"

"LaVerne and LaVilla would like to get to know you better, but they have one very firm rule about the gentlemen they date. They're a competitive pair, you see, and they never, ever go out with someone who has beaten them at tennis."

"Ah." An amused smile curled Stefan's lips. "It seems you are offering me a most creative bribe to throw a match."

"We men have to stick together."

"That is often true."

"The twins happen to be available tonight, if you don't have any other plans."

Sliding a glance toward the waiting twins, Stefan's smile grew broader. "A most enticing offer."

"They're nice girls, Stefan, so don't go getting any weird ideas," Curt emphasized, his protective instincts leaping to the forefront. "We're just talking about dinner and dancing. That's it."

"And you, my young friend, is that all you have in mind for Kathryn?"

"For starters." Curt figured it would take more than one date to get past all of Kathryn's self-defense mechanisms. But in the long run, the final outcome would be well worth the effort. "She's special, Stefan. I know that, and there's not a chance in hell I'd take advantage of her. Not when push comes to shove. What comes next will be the lady's choice."

"Gentlemen," Kathryn called. "Are we going to play tennis sometime today or just chat?"

Stefan paused a moment, then nodding, he extended his hand to Curt to bind the agreement. "I shall look forward to a most delightful, *circumspect* evening. As I am sure you will, too."

"I'd rather Kathryn doesn't realize what's going on."

"I shall be the soul of discretion, my young friend."

Flexing his shoulder muscles and twirling his racquet confidently, Curt took up a position behind the baseline. "You can have the first serve," he shouted. "It's only fair since I did the challenging."

"As you wish," Stefan agreed, tossing two balls to Kathryn. "You may begin, my dear."

Kathryn held the first ball in her hand and looked across the court at a waiting Curt. The poor guy— forget his spiffy white shorts and incredibly muscular legs—was going to lose so badly she almost felt sorry for him. But not quite. After all, he'd brought this on himself. However, a niggling bit of conscience forced her to make one concession.

"Curt, it's okay if you want to play right-handed," she said. "I won't hold you to that part of the bargain. Either way, it's not likely to make much difference."

"That's all right, sweetheart. The fact is, I always play tennis left-handed."

Kathryn's jaw tightened as the sudden picture of Curt eating lunch came to her, his fork in his *left* hand. The no-account masher had conned her again!

She tossed the ball in the air, acing the serve with all of the murderous fury she felt. She and Stefan were going to cream Curt and his pretty harem girls two sets to zip, or she'd know the reason why.

KATHRYN DIDN'T KNOW WHY the game was going so badly.

She and Stefan had lost the first set six-two, and were already behind four-one in the second set. Stefan didn't seem to be moving as fast as he should after the outside shots, and every time a volley landed between them, they messed up each other's timing. She'd never imagined a former pro would serve quite so many double faults in what amounted to a recreational game.

Of course, Curt was a pretty formidable player for an amateur. Exceptionally agile for a big man, she thought. He was a thinking player who knew where to place his shots to best advantage. He often forced their errors with an unexpected dink, or managed to send a shot right down the alley. And the twins were as fresh as sparkling daisies, she thought unkindly, watching them alternate play every few games.

Meanwhile, Kathryn was beginning to droop like a wilted dandelion, more so with each lost point.

Perhaps Stefan's age was finally beginning to catch up with him. She knew hers was.

What about the bet? she fretted as she dived for the ball and missed with her backhand. Her knee stung as it scraped against concrete. How could she possibly make good on their wager if Curt won the match?

Dragging herself up from where she had sprawled on the court, she gritted her teeth and renewed her determination. The match wasn't over until the last point was played.

"Hey, how 'bout we take a breather," Curt suggested.

"Only if Stefan wants a break," Kathryn replied grimly, lining up in front of the net to wait for Curt's serve to her partner. "I'm fine."

"Stiff upper lip, my dear. We'll have them on the run soon."

That didn't happen. Stefan muffed the next return, and Kathryn was so arm weary she couldn't handle the one after that, giving Curt and LaVerne a five-one lead in the set.

Oddly, when Stefan took his turn serving, he seemed rejuvenated, a new man who refused to allow defeat. Four quick aces and Kathryn's hopes flared, only to be shattered again when they lost the next game, set and match.

Kathryn collapsed on a bench at the side of the tennis court. She leaned back against the chain-link fence to let the breeze dry the perspiration from her face. The air currents from the sea swept up toward the Hollywood Hills, cleansing the Los Angeles basin of smog. She closed her eyes, and her thoughts, against the dreadful tennis match. Things could not have gone more wrong.

Someone wiped her face with a cool damp cloth, a gentle gesture almost sensual in its tenderness. She caught the scent of clean male sweat and the spicy aroma of after-shave. At some other level she was aware of a monotonous thumping noise, which she assumed was her heart slowing its beat. Carefully she opened her eyes to meet blue-green ones gazing back at her. *The winner.* Curt Creighton.

She stifled a groan. He was close, really close. His hair was dark with sweat and his breath warm across the cool path he stroked with the damp cloth. His nearness invited a woman to caress his cheek, or finger comb his mussed hair back into place. His full lips were slightly parted, shaped to induce a woman to explore further with her own.

Fighting temptation, Kathryn refused the unspoken invitation.

"You okay?" he asked with what appeared to be sincerity.

"Wonderful." She would have felt equally content if she'd been asked to walk across a bed of hot coals.

"You played a heck of a good game."

"Right. I guess that's why we lost."

"It just wasn't your day."

"Or Stefan's." She looked around, past the swimming pool and the neatly landscaped grounds, suddenly aware that her partner was no longer in sight. Nor were the sexy twins. The thumping noise of her heart accelerated. "Where is everyone?"

"They had other things to do." He slid the cloth to the back of her neck, lifting her ponytail as he rubbed the soft terry fabric along her flesh.

"Oh." Her throat constricted around the word. Ending up alone with Curt had not been part of Kathryn's plan. Her *failed* plan, she mentally corrected.

"You brought your own car, didn't you?"

She nodded, too intrigued by the sinuous movement of cool cloth against her overheated, sensitive skin to speak. Fascinated, too, by the tiny gold flecks she could see in Curt's aqua eyes, and the sweep of his unfairly long lashes. The beat of her heart grew louder, so insistent she finally realized the noise wasn't her heart but something outside...

Her head snapped up.

A helicopter hovered right above the tennis court, the spinning blades blurred against the bright blue sky.

"Isn't that guy flying awfully low?" she asked.

Curt shifted his position to prevent the turbulent wind the rotors kicked up from blowing dust in Kathryn's face. "Uh, it must be a training flight," he explained, shouting to be heard as he curled his body protectively over hers.

"Have you complained to the FAA? This is no place for a student pilot to be practicing. What if he had engine trouble?"

The corners of Curt's lips twitched into a smile. "I'll have my attorney look into the matter."

"Good idea. I'll have a letter to the FAA ready for Tom's signature by the end of work on Monday. You shouldn't have to put up with that kind of a hazard in a residential neighborhood. Particularly an exclusive area like this. Surely you and your neighbors have political clout."

"Yeah, well, it doesn't happen often."

Kathryn watched as the helicopter finally moved on and blessed quiet returned. Into that silent vacuum came a new awareness. Curt had one arm draped casually around her shoulder, and his other hand rested...warmly...intimately...on her bare thigh. In bemused surprise, she studied the contrast in textures between his hard, masculine hand and her softer flesh. She imagined how the hand that had gripped his tennis racquet so surely and powerfully would feel caressing a sensitive path along her inner thigh. In response to that vividly tactile image, she felt a clenching and tightening low in her body, an uncoiling of longing that brought moisture to the apex between her legs.

The nearly forgotten sensation of pure, unadulterated lust drove Kathryn to her feet in a near panic.

"If everyone else is gone, I'd better be on my way, too." With shaking hands, she slid her racquet into its carrying case.

"No rush."

"I've got a ton of studying to do. Exams next week." Keeping her head down, she refused to meet his gaze. She knew what he'd see in her eyes. Desire. A primitive urge she'd spent years repressing, and which Curt had rekindled as easily as if he'd struck a match to summer-dry grass. *Damn.* She never should have agreed to see him, even in a crowd.

"Okay. If you've gotta go now, that's fine. I'll pick you up at seven."

She whirled around to face him. "No." The word came out as a painful croak.

"Come on, honey. You're not going to welch on our bet, are you?"

"Not tonight," she pleaded. Not when she was feeling so vulnerable, so very tempted by Curt's charming smile and the residual warmth of where he had placed his hand. She felt hot all over, her lungs hyperventilating at the least little provocation.

"Tomorrow, then?"

"That's a work night," she hedged. "I never go out on work nights."

In a deceptively smooth gesture, Curt extended his arms to trap her between the chain-link fence and his hard, unyielding chest. His face was only inches from hers, so close their lips were almost touching. "I'm not going to take no for an answer because I know you'd hate yourself in the morning for reneging on an honest bet. And I won't have that on my conscience." His voice dropped to a low, persuasive tone. "Name the day, sweet Katie."

She felt the color drain from her face. "Please don't call me that." *Please don't remind me of my foolish adolescent mistakes.*

"You don't like Katie? It fits you better than Kathryn, it seems to me."

"The name brings back... Let's just say I attach some rather unpleasant memories to that particular nickname." Memories that included being the subject of gossip in the town of Waverly, hurtful words from her father and the knowledge that someday soon she had to face her past. The phone call to her sister had been a beginning. But only that.

He twirled the tips of her hair between his fingers, slowly, seductively. "What we're doing here, Katie girl, is making memories for the future. *Our* future. Nothing that happened before we met makes a fig of difference in the grand scheme of things. Can you understand that?"

Unable to verbalize a response, or shake off the memories that had haunted her for so long, she shook her head. History couldn't be forgotten.

"So about our date. How 'bout next Saturday?" he persisted. "After your exams are over. We'll make a day of it."

In the worst way she wanted to decline. But she'd made the bet in good faith and her basic sense of honesty and fair play required her to pay it off. The fact that she and Stefan should have won the tennis match hands down didn't matter. They'd lost. Badly. And now she'd have to pay the price. Her only hope was in the next seven days she'd be able to steel herself against Curt's determined assault on her reason.

Numbly she nodded.

A victorious smile creased Curt's cheeks. "Great. I'll pick you up at ten Saturday morning. Dress for a picnic and bring along a change of clothes for dinner."

He dipped his head and brushed her lips in a quick kiss that sealed the bargain and took her breath away. Her lips tingling, she stared up at him, prepared to announce her disapproval in no uncertain terms. But the words wouldn't slide past the constriction of her throat. Lord, she was in trouble. Deep trouble.

The sound of a woman's voice jarred Kathryn back to some sense of reality.

"Well, hi, you two. Looks like the game is just getting under way."

She was young and pretty, with flyaway brown hair, and she wore a vibrantly colored costume that made her look like a modern-day gypsy. Not very tall, her silver bracelets jingled as she scampered across the tennis court, her earrings catching the slanting rays of sunlight like colorful mirrors. When she stood on tiptoe to give Curt a kiss on the cheek,

Kathryn barely suppressed a violent urge to sock the young woman in the kisser.

"Didn't mean to interrupt your playtime, big brother," the woman said, her grin an impish replica of Curt's.

His sister! The steam quickly went out of Kathryn's jealous fury. What on earth was wrong with her? Jealousy had never been her style. And she certainly had no claim on Curt—nor did she want any.

Curt linked his arm around his sister's waist. "Go easy, Lucy. Kathryn Prim is a very serious lady."

"Really?" Lucy extended her hand in friendly welcome. "I hope you're also smart enough to keep my brother in line."

"I doubt anyone can do that," Kathryn said with a shake of her head. She'd certainly failed to keep him in line, Kathryn realized. Or perhaps she only lacked the ability to keep her own fantasies under control. Curt was the kind of man she'd never dared dream about, and didn't want to deal with. By his nearness alone he conjured up too many erotic images, needs she'd tucked so far to the back of her awareness she was sure she'd forgotten them—until now.

Lucy slipped her arm through Kathryn's, firmly ushering her away from the tennis court and toward the house. "Well, come on inside. I'll make us a pitcher of apple-cinnamon herbal tea that tastes so good it's downright decadent, and we'll talk a little girl talk. I know all there is to know about Curt."

"You do not," he objected.

"Important things like where he's ticklish," she continued.

"Hey, that's not fair." Curt maneuvered to keep up with his sister's quick pace.

"And how he gets really upset if anyone messes with his toothpaste."

"I only got mad because you left the damn cap off and the stuff got all over the clothes in my suitcase. I had an important appointment."

"You had a date, and she was a dog."

"Now wait a minute..."

Kathryn stifled a smile as she and Lucy left Curt in their wake, him mumbling something about taking a shower if he wasn't appreciated by the fairer sex. She'd forgotten the *joys* of sibling rivalry, the way her little sister, Alice, had been such a pest, and how Kathryn had loved her.

In this case, brother and sister obviously shared the same irrepressible charm. She envied Lucy's vivacious personality and her easy confidence, characteristics Kathryn sorely lacked. However, it was time to clear up any misunderstanding.

Once in the kitchen, Lucy shooed Marvin, the butler, away so she could make the tea herself. She had so much effervescent energy, she seemed to move in fast forward, exhausting Kathryn even as she watched in admiration and amazement.

"Now tell me about you and my brother," she said, dropping ice cubes into a pitcher of ruby red tea.

"There's nothing to tell."

"But I saw you two in a clench out on the tennis court. I just assumed..."

Kathryn bristled. "It was not a clench," she said tightly. "He was simply..." Seducing her, or trying to.

"He kissed you."

"Well, yes, but that doesn't mean anything."

Slowing her pace, Lucy set the pitcher on the kitchen table and poured two glasses of tea. "You mean you're not... seeing Curt?"

"No. Absolutely not." Realizing her denial had been too vehement, Kathryn gratefully took a drink of the tea in order to calm down. "I mean, well, we do have a date next weekend. But that's all. It's only because I work for the firm representing him in the Roslyn Kellogg matter."

"Oh, that." Lucy wrinkled her nose. "Boy, did I misjudge her."

"Yes, that does happen. So you see, my relationship with Curt—Mr. Creighton—is really strictly business."

The young woman looked at Kathryn with a fair amount of skepticism. "Pity. I was hoping..." Turning away, Lucy popped open a cabinet and retrieved a can of cashews, which she placed on the table. "See, I think Curt is kind of lonesome—"

"Your brother? Lonely?" Kathryn nearly choked on the words. "That hardly seems possible when he has the Radisson twins to keep him company. Among others, I assume."

"Oh, they don't mean anything to Curt. None of the girls I stash here until I can find them some decent acting roles are his type. In fact, the problem Curt has is finding somebody who isn't interested in him just for his money, or what he can do for them." She popped a couple of nuts in her mouth and chewed thoughtfully. "I guess I've kinda got the same problem. Comes with the territory, I suppose." With a jingle of her bracelets, Lucy made an expansive gesture that took in the largest, best-equipped kitchen Kathryn had ever seen, with its miles of stainless steel and butcher block countertops. It made a mockery of her entire apartment. What she'd seen of the rest of the house was equally extravagant, sparing no expense.

Kathryn had never considered the unique problems of the truly wealthy. Finding a lifetime partner was an iffy matter, at best. Complicated by money, the odds of meeting someone who loved you for yourself—not your savings account, stocks and assorted other investments—would certainly make a person wary.

None of that explained why Curt was coming on to her in an all-out sensual attack.

Nor did the thought ease the persistent headache that nagged at the back of Kathryn's skull. Sometime during the next seven days, she was going to have to come up with a viable excuse to cancel her date with Curt Creighton. To do otherwise would be to put her heart, as well as her mental well-being, at far too great a risk.

Chapter Six

Blurry eyed from a third straight night of restless sleep—ever since she had agreed to a date with Curt Creighton—Kathryn peered into the bathroom mirror. She opened her mouth wide and prayed to find some sign of infection at the back of her throat. Just her luck, she hadn't caught whatever it was that had kept her office mate, Clarence, out of work for a week. She'd do anything to be able to cancel out on Curt.

"Coward!" she accused her image.

She could fake a broken leg, she mused as she splashed cold water on her face. Crutches and a little plaster of paris would do the trick. Of course, Curt would probably counter with her very own gold-plated wheelchair. He was not an easy man to discourage.

On the other hand, she could try for a restraining order, though she doubted any court in the country could contain Curt's persistence or his sexy grin.

How the devil was she supposed to concentrate on her work—or her exams—with Curt so completely filling her mind? She never should have accepted his challenge and the wager, even though she'd been absolutely sure Stefan could beat Curt blindfolded. The unexpected loss of the tennis match still puzzled her.

A half hour later, as she was picking up her purse to leave for the office, there was a knock on the door.

"Ah, *chérie,* I was afraid something was wrong. You are late leaving for your place of employment and you are usually so prompt."

"I know." She smiled at her neighbor's concern. Living across the hall from Rudy was like having a doting grandfather nearby. "I had some trouble sleeping last night."

"My poor dear," he said, slipping into his Dr. Welby imitation, "losing sleep is a serious problem. You must see me in my office later and I will prescribe a cure."

Kathryn knew the cure—get Curt Creighton out of her life. Just how she could manage that, she didn't know. Unless...

Her mind racing, she considered a near-impossible scheme that had at least a slender chance of success.

"Rudy, have you ever met my boss, Tom Weston?"

"*Oui,* it was on a Saturday when we stopped by your office. We were on our way to a matinee, as I recall."

"Yes, of course. I'd almost forgotten." She mentally crossed her fingers. "Would it be possible for you to imitate Tom's voice."

He hesitated a moment, then seemed to grow in stature as he took on the role of a successful attorney. "Kathryn, would you mind bringing me the file on the Smith case?" His voice carefully modulated, he straighten his imaginary tie. "When you have a moment."

"Yes! That's perfect." She gave him an impetuous hug. "Oh, Rudy, I need a favor. A really big favor."

"Of course, *mon amie.* What is it you wish?"

AT THE SOUND of the phone, Curt set aside the applications for grant requests he'd been reading. The Mollie Creighton Foundation, named for his mother, funded a lot of charitable projects across the country, and he liked to make sure they were ones that would make an impact on some pretty tough problems.

"Creighton here."

"Hello, Curt, it's Tom Weston."

"How's it going, buddy."

"Everything's fine in terms of your case. But Kathryn asked me to call you."

Thoughts of accidents or dire illness caused Curt to frown. "What's wrong?"

"I'm afraid she won't be able to make your date this weekend."

Letting his feet slide off the open desk drawer where they had been propped, Curt asked, "How come?"

"My fault, I'm afraid. There's a seminar this weekend on the legal ramifications of artificial intelligence. I need her to attend."

His frown deepened into a scowl. "All weekend?" Very convenient, it occurred to Curt, but not entirely believable.

"Sessions go from early morning until late at night. You know how these business things go. She's very sorry, of course."

"Of course." Curt's instincts told him something wasn't quite right. "How come she didn't call me?"

"She was afraid you would think she was only making an excuse."

She had that damn straight. Curt had been looking forward to the weekend a great deal. If it hadn't been his old friend calling... Then again, Kathryn wouldn't be above... There was that nosy neighbor that lived across the hall...

An internal alarm sounded in Curt's head. Over his lifetime a lot of people had tried to con him for one reason or another—usually money. He'd developed some pretty good instincts that, while they weren't necessarily foolproof—as evidenced by Roslyn Kellogg—had prevented him from squandering the wealth he'd inherited.

Money, he suspected, wasn't the problem this time.

Thoughtfully he rubbed his palm along his jaw. "Hey, Tom, I saw Henry Sampson the other day. Remember him?"

"Sure. Who could forget ol' Henry? How is he?"

"He's still as skinny as a rail. Hasn't gained a pound since we graduated."

"Is that a fact?" The person on the other end of the line cleared his throat, but Curt had already learned all he needed to know. Hank Sampson was a three-hundred-pound offensive lineman for the Rams. "I have another call. We'll talk later."

"Sure. Tell Kathryn I'll give her a call." Soon. Very soon.

"That won't be necessary. She's really very busy."

"Not too busy for me." Smiling, Curt quietly cradled the phone. Kathryn Prim was one shrewd lady. She just hadn't learned yet how early she'd have to get up in the morning in order to keep ahead of him.

He imagined she wouldn't be at all pleased when she learned how she'd lost the tennis match. Confessing that particular sin would require delicate timing.

"NICE TRY, PRETTY LADY. A convenient weekend seminar? Very clever."

Kathryn cringed at the sound of Curt's voice even as his compellingly masculine image flooded her awareness. Damn these direct phone lines! In the future, she wanted all of her calls screened.

"What do you want?" she asked, as if she didn't know. Clearly Rudy's acting skills weren't as good as she had hoped.

"Who'd you have make the call?" he asked, his amused tone bringing to mind sexy blue-green eyes crinkled at the corners with a smile. "That scrawny guy who lives across the hall from you? He's not half-bad as an actor. Had me going there awhile."

"Curt, I really can't make our date on Saturday."

"Sure you can."

"No. Really. I've got to..." He sounded so close on the phone, as though he were in her office; she could almost smell his spicy after-shave. "It's the only day I can do my grocery shopping."

"You can do better than that, sweetheart."

If only he were right, she thought, frantically searching for a new excuse. "I mean my shopping and enrolling for next semester. You know how long those registration lines can be."

"Register by mail. Saves a lot of time."

She rolled her eyes. Arguing with Curt Creighton was like trying to tap dance through a mine field. "Would you believe I have an aunt in East Angola? She's a missionary and she's been very ill. I have to go see the dear woman one last time."

"Good girl. You're getting more creative by the minute."

A smile tugged at her lips. Impossible man. "I have an appointment to give blood. You wouldn't want me to miss that."

"You can reschedule. I'll arrange a mobile van just for you, if I have to."

He would. He'd probably buy the damn thing. "Really, Curt, I think I'm coming down with something. The flu, maybe."

A large, very masculine hand with tapered fingers and a smattering of cinnamon brown hair on the back reached across Kathryn's desk and pressed the button on her phone to disconnect the call.

Kathryn's head snapped up. He was there. In her office. All six foot two of him, leather jacket, silver belt buckle and helmet included. Her heart did some sort of impossible somersault and air lodged painfully in her lungs.

He flipped his cellular phone closed. "Honey, the only thing you've got is an acute case of cold feet."

"Good Lord, you scared me half to death. I could have had a heart attack." As it was, her heart was thudding so fast it felt as if a jackhammer had taken up residence in her chest. "Besides, you shouldn't be here. You promised you wouldn't embarrass—"

"I'm seeing Tom. The one who's your boss, remember? No one's going to think anything about me stopping by to say hello to the paralegal who is working on my case."

She leveled her eyebrows into her most intimidating glower, which she knew wouldn't do a damn bit of good. "You must have gone through the line *twice* when they were passing out chutzpah."

He winked. "Saturday. As planned. Ten o'clock sharp."

As he vanished out the door, Kathryn sank back into her chair. About the only thing left to do was to give herself a big dose of food poisoning come Friday night. But she didn't think she could go through with that. Besides, there were moments—not many, she assured herself—when she actually *liked* sparring with Curt Creighton. She never would have imagined it would be so much fun to challenge a man with her wits.

"A PLANE?"

"Sure. It's the fastest way I know to get to Pebble Beach."

"Pebble..." Kathryn choked on the name of their destination, an exclusive resort community three hundred miles up the California coast. Waiting like a silver magic carpet on the tarmac at the Santa Monica airport, the private jet was so sleek it looked as if it was flying a million miles an hour just sitting still. It had been hard enough for Kathryn to accept a uniformed Marvin as the chauffeur of the mile-long limousine Curt had picked her up in. Now she found herself facing a liveried crew wearing the corporate colors of Creighton Enterprises—an appropriate combination of silver, gold and U.S. mint green.

She shook her head in total amazement. "I thought we'd probably go to a park for a picnic," she protested weakly.

"Too ordinary." Curt cupped her elbow as he escorted her up the steps into the plane's cabin. He handed off her hanging bag with her change of clothes to one of the smiling crew members and briefly introduced her to the pilot, Walter Jackson.

The plush interior made the plane look like a corporate conference room—thick carpeting, swivel chairs upholstered in rich velour and a matching couch along one side of the cabin. Kathryn detected a faint scent of newness to the aircraft, along with a trace of lemon air freshener...and wealth. Every time she was with Curt she caught the seductive scent of megadollars spent as casually as she might spend a little spare change.

"You don't do things halfway, do you?" she asked, allowing Curt to seat her on the couch.

"Creighton Enterprises has interests all over the world. Europe. The Orient. South America. My top managers need to be able to respond to a crisis without having to wait for an airline."

"Besides that, you really like having expensive toys."

A guilty grin creased both of his cheeks. "What would be the point of having money if you couldn't spend it?" he admitted.

"None, I guess."

He sat down beside her and stretched out his long legs, crossing his ankles one over the other. His scruffy sandals, cutoff jeans and cropped T-shirt were the antithesis of dress for success, yet she couldn't imagine a more powerful, virile man. A light coating of swirling hair roughened his muscular thighs—tanned thighs a woman instinctively wanted to touch. His ribbed belly invited an even more intimate caress. He was definitely the kind of man who would turn heads in a nunnery.

Kathryn would somehow have to endure more than twelve hours in his company without revealing just how strongly he affected her. A formidable task when she could already feel her breathing accelerating and her breasts growing heavier by the moment.

A crewman pulled the cabin door closed and the Fasten Seat Belt sign lit up. The engines whined as they turned over. Deep in the pit of her stomach, Kathryn felt a fluttery sensation that had little to do with a fear of flying.

Chapter Seven

A little more than two hours later, Curt sat on the beach drizzling a handful of white sand through his fingers. He and Kathryn had consumed about half the generous amount of food and fine wine provided by the country-club hotel for their picnic. Leaning back in the low beach chair, he felt content, well fed and ready to make his move.

"I don't know about you, but it seems to me this beats the hell out of balance sheets and corporate maneuvering."

"You sound like a man who's not happy with his work."

She was kneeling on the corner of the blanket, putting away the leftovers in the wicker picnic basket, a picture of domestic concentration. Her paisley print sundress revealed creamy smooth shoulders; her arms and hands moved with the grace of a dancer. Curt wished he had thought to bring his camera along. The dappled sunlight beneath the cypress tree fascinated him as it caressed Kathryn's fair complexion, first at one delicate juncture and then another. He'd like his kisses to be able to play tag with the traveling dollops of sunlight.

"It's lonely at the top," he said, trying for a long-suffering tone. "All those people relying on you to make the right decisions. The stress can really get to you."

"Why don't you quit?"

He scowled. She was supposed to be sympathizing with the sacrifices he was forced to make, not finding an easy solution to his imaginary problems. "And throw all those people to the wolves? I couldn't do that."

"It seems to me if your companies are so successful, a good many corporations would be happy to buy you out. You could retire."

"But then it wouldn't be Creighton Enterprises anymore," he stubbornly countered. "My dad started the company."

"Being happy with what you do is important."

"Well, yeah..."

"Exactly what is it you do for the company?" Kathryn asked, suddenly very curious about the man who was so persistent in his pursuit of her.

In his thoughtful pause before answering, she detected a change in his cavalier attitude, as though he took his business activities far more seriously than she had suspected.

"Lucy and I are majority shareholders. Making decisions is about the extent of my involvement. We have a very competent CEO—Arnold Beaman—who handles the day-to-day operations."

"What sort of decisions do you make?"

Gazing out to sea, he appeared to weigh his answer, and she sensed an intelligent mind that examined issues with the same care as an appellate judge. "Last week Arnie came to me with this idea to shut down a small plant we operate in Alabama. I nixed the deal."

"Why?"

He shrugged as though the decision was of no consequence. "The place employs about a hundred and twenty people making fancy lingerie for our Seduction catalog. The whole town has a population of maybe two thousand. If we closed the plant and moved the operation to Taiwan, like Arnie wanted to, it would kill the town's economy."

"But wouldn't the move have made good sense in terms of profit?"

"Sure. That's why Arnie suggested it. He's always watching the bottom line—which makes him a dynamite CEO. Sometimes, though, he forgets there are people involved. That little town was where my mother grew up. Two generations of folks have worked in that factory. I figure we owe them our loyalty."

Curt's revelation knocked Kathryn back on her mental haunches. She hadn't expected him to be the corporate conscience of Creighton Enterprises. That was a whole different image than the one portrayed in the tabloids. A very appealing one, she admitted.

Shifting his position to the corner of the blanket opposite Kathryn, Curt picked up the wine bottle and poured each of them a fresh glass. He hadn't intended to talk about business. That wasn't something a guy intent on romancing a woman was supposed to bring up. But Kathryn had seemed curious, and he admitted to being flattered by her interest.

"Are you happy working for Weston?" he asked.

"Mostly. The firm is fair with its employees and the people I work with are nice." She accepted the wine, but didn't immediately sip from the glass. "I'll like the actual work even more after I pass the bar."

"You're that ambitious?"

"I'm not sure it's so much ambition as it is a desire to be independent."

"Independent," he echoed under his breath. "That's not exactly the answer a guy wants to hear."

She visibly stiffened. "You don't approve of a woman being self-reliant?"

"Of course I do. Careers for women are fine. It's just that..." He speared his fingers through his hair. With Kathryn he always seemed to be a little off balance, not nearly as self-confident as he was with other women. What could he say now? He'd been idly wondering if marriage and family were important to her. That kind of question would really be sticking his neck out.

For now he'd be better off with a neutral topic.

"How 'bout a walk along the beach?" He levered himself to his feet.

"Should we take the picnic basket back to the hotel?"

"This is a private beach. They'll take care of things."

"The hotel manager seemed to know you pretty well."

"I've played a few rounds of golf here over the years."

Kathryn guessed it had been more frequent than that. The two men had been quite cordial, with the manager showing Curt considerable deference. "Yes, I can see being a corporate mogul is an onerous task," she teased. "So stressful and exhausting."

He gave her an innocent look that didn't quite reach his eyes.

Smiling, she stood and brushed the sand from her skirt. In a way, Curt reminded her of a sixth-grade boy intent on impressing his first girl. He needn't bother. She had already moved beyond impressed to seriously attracted. He simply didn't understand that a picnic at the local park would have created the same feelings.

On the other hand, she couldn't help wondering how long it would take a person to get used to the perks wealthy people took in stride. Your own airplane. A private beach on a nearly deserted stretch of sand. Servants and hotel managers at your beck and call. With an effort, Kathryn repressed that secret part of her that would love the chance to adjust to extravagant living. Little wonder, after surviving on her own for twelve years, she might be lured by such luxury.

When they reached the edge of the water, she slipped off her sandals and carried them dangling by the straps. The moist sand pressed through her toes, the breeze fluttered her skirt gently against her bare legs and flicked the lose strands of her hair against her cheek like the hurried kiss of a lover. Hypnotically the waves rolled up the beach to leave a curving rim of white foam that quickly vanished. Kathryn wasn't sure when Curt had taken her free hand in his. She simply knew within the sensual play of sound, sight and texture, his warm hand stood out as the strength she wanted to hold on to. But she didn't dare think about that.

A towheaded child of about six came running backward down the beach, dragging a kite that kicked and bounced along the sand.

"Whoa, young fella," Curt said, scooping the boy off his feet before he could crash into them. "What's your hurry?"

The child's legs freewheeled in midair. "I'm flying my kite."

"Funny, I thought kites where supposed to go up in the sky, not bounce along the sand."

"My mom's boyfriend said I hadda run real fast a real long way. Then it'll go up all by itself. He said so."

A quick glance down the length of the beach made it clear to Kathryn that the boyfriend had something else on his mind besides flying kites. By now the child was well out of shouting range of his mother, assuming she ever bothered to check on his whereabouts. Kathryn felt a twist of anger at the woman's negligence, followed by a sense of longing that was almost as painful.

"We'd better walk the boy back to his mother," she suggested, fighting the sudden tightness in her throat.

"I don't think she's real interested in maternal activities right now," Curt said grimly. "My father had some lady friends after Mom died who shared the same view."

"I wanna fly my kite."

Kathryn's gaze met Curt's aqua eyes, and she watched as a moment of sorrow was replaced by a contagious spark of mischief.

"I used to be pretty good at this kite-flying business," he said. "How 'bout you?"

"I don't think I've ever flown a kite. My father never had time to—"

"Say no more." Curt knelt in front of the boy. "What's your name, kid?"

The child puffed out his bare little chest. "Paul Carter Cogswell Maguire the third, sir."

"That's quite a mouthful."

"It's the same name as my dad 'cept he's number two. He doesn't live with us no more but I can spell our whole name. *P...A...U...*"

"I'll tell you what, Paul Carter Cogswell Maguire the third, how'd you like to help me teach this nice lady how to fly a kite?"

The child's expression clouded over. "I'm not real sure I can."

With his hand, Curt ruffled the boy's hair. "You'll do fine."

Curt retrieved the bright red-and-yellow kite, then made a quick inspection of the crosspieces, taking a moment to adjust the tension on the bowstring.

"She looks sound to me," he announced. "Katie, I want you to walk the kite about fifty feet that way." He indicated a direction opposite the water's edge. "Hold the kite up. When you feel me tug on the string, let go."

"You mean I don't have to race up and down the beach like Paul was?" she said with a laugh.

"Not in this kind of a breeze." As though to emphasize the strength of the currents, the wind kicked a lock of Curt's hair down over his forehead, giving him a devilishly attractive, boyish appearance.

"I gets to hold the string," Paul insisted.

"You bet, kid. As soon as I get her up there for you."

Kathryn paced off the distance as instructed. Turning, she watched Curt and the little boy with their heads together, conferring so seriously they might have been debating the merits of a new stock investment. An ache tightened in her chest and the sharp breeze off the ocean suddenly made her eyes water. Curt, she realized, would make a wonderful father. Heavy corporate responsibilities or not, he hadn't yet outgrown the ability to have fun. Somewhere along the way she'd certainly lost the knack.

She wondered if she could relearn the gift of easy laughter, the joy of innocence...with the right teacher.

"You ready?" Curt called to her.

She swallowed uncomfortably. Ready for kite flying, yes, but she wasn't so sure about the rest. "Whenever you are."

"'Atta girl!"

At the tug of the string, she released the kite. It rose a few feet, dipped precariously, then caught the breeze once again. As Curt let out more line the kite soared upward. Smiling, Kathryn craned her neck to watch its flight. The kite shrank in size until the red and yellow colors blended into a bright orange.

"My turn! My turn!" Paul insisted.

"Okay, son, but you've got to hold on tight. We don't want to let her get away from us."

Kathryn strolled back to join the master kite flyer and his eager young apprentice. Standing at the boy's side, unobtrusively holding the string for safety's sake, Curt let Paul fly the kite until the child became impatient standing in one place for so long.

"I wanna run with it some more," the child announced.

"In a minute, son. First we've got to give Katie a turn," Curt said. "Is that okay?"

For the second time that afternoon, Kathryn didn't put up a fuss when Curt called her Katie. Maybe, for the moment, the sea breeze had blown her bad memories away.

With a shrug, the child relinquished his grip on the string, then danced around in the sand to let out some of his pent-up energy.

Kathryn took control, surprised by the powerful pull of the kite, acutely aware of Curt standing so close to her. His hand held hers and his body brushed against her shoulder, his thigh against her hip. His spicy after-shave mixed with the scent of the sea, a seductively masculine combination.

When he slid his free arm around her midriff, Kathryn's breath caught. The warmth of his lips feathered tiny shivery kisses on the side of her neck, sending waves of desire curling through her body. She shuddered with each new cascading swirl of pleasure, instinctively leaning back against the warmth of Curt's body.

And all the time the beautiful dancing kite tugged at her, luring Kathryn to follow its lead to freedom, in much the same way Curt tempted her to reach beyond the rigid limits she'd set for herself. But she knew where that temptation could lead . . . to heartbreak and loneliness.

"Curt." His name was little more than a husky whisper, and she cleared her throat of the tightness she felt. "It's getting late. I think we'd better get Paul back to his mother."

"She hasn't seemed very interested in the boy so far."

"I know." Kathryn removed Curt's arm from around her waist and eased herself away from his strong male physique. At the sudden absence of the heat radiating from his body, gooseflesh rose on her arms. "It's getting cold, too. We'd better call it a day."

"It'll take me a few minutes to reel in the kite." He studied her with eyes darkened with the same desire she had felt. A desire she refused to acknowledge. "You'll wait?" he asked.

She nodded. If she had good sense, she ought to either take the next commercial flight back home, or go for a very long, cold swim in the ocean to cool down her raging hormones. But something about Curt Creighton always managed to dull her wits. A truly intelligent woman never would have agreed to this date in the first place.

THEY RETURNED PAUL to his mother, who seemed surprised to learn the boy had even been missing. Then Kathryn and Curt went back to the hotel and settled down in the cozy, well-appointed bar for a drink. Not quite trusting herself sober, much less tipsy, Kathryn stuck with a designer water. Curt had a beer.

As the dinner hour approached, Curt announced that their rooms were ready.

"Rooms?" Kathryn questioned suspiciously.

"So we can change for dinner."

"Oh." He'd obviously thought through all the details, and probably had additional plans for the rooms later.

"*Separate* rooms," he stated in response to her troubled frown. "Adjoining, of course."

"How convenient."

"With a locked door between them. If that's your choice."

"It's one of my hard-and-fast rules." Padlocks, dead bolts and a six-inch-thick metal bar would just about do the trick. He was too damn tempting, too completely sure of himself and far too accurate in his assessment of her reaction.

As usual, his amused smile did fluttery things to her midsection. "I gather you don't trust me."

"Not a chance, fella."

The low rumble of his laughter invited company and made Kathryn think about hot chocolate and long winter nights wrapped in a warm blanket in front of a crackling fire. Homey things. Loving things. Things a woman longed for in the secret darkness of night. Futilely, she fought a responding smile and the heat that suffused her body.

SHE WAS STILL FEELING that same heat after dinner as Curt smiled at her across the small table for two in a secluded corner of the restaurant. His white dinner jacket emphasized his ruddy good looks and made his shoulders appear even broader than usual. Every female eye in the room had turned in his direction when they'd entered the dining room, and a good many of the women, escorted or not, had pointedly glanced in his direction as the evening progressed.

To Kathryn's surprise, Curt didn't return a single flirtatious invitation. The fact that he had eyes only for her gave Kathryn a sense of feminine pleasure she'd rarely experienced.

"Have I mentioned how beautiful you look this evening?" he asked, casually covering her hand with his.

"Several times," she reminded him.

"I wouldn't want to overlook an important detail like that."

"I'm sure you wouldn't." Every detail of the evening had been exquisitely planned. The single red rose at her place at the table. Soft, romantic music. A discreet waiter constantly filling her wineglass with a smooth vintage that left her feeling light-headed. A delicious meal of delicately flavored fish and crisp sautéed vegetables with a savory pilaf. All of that followed by giant strawberries dipped in sinfully rich chocolate. Kathryn was beginning to think Curt was working his way through Seduction Incorporated's catalog of tricks page by page. Worse yet, she was succumbing to his charms.

"I like the way a few hours in the sun brings out your freckles," he commented.

"They're the bane of my life. I wish I could cover them but no makeup works."

"Oh, no, you mustn't hide them. I particularly don't want you to cover this one." He lightly touched his fingertip to the bridge of her nose. "That one's my favorite."

"Don't be ridiculous."

"Hmm. Maybe you're right." He studied her so seriously, Kathryn almost laughed aloud. "Perhaps this one," he concluded, his finger skimming across her cheek to an alternate freckle. "Then again, I find your lips quite fascinating, too." His exploring finger trailed a slow path to the new subject of his conversation.

Kathryn shuddered as he rasped his finger along the shape of her lower lip. Her mouth opened instinctively, and she tasted the remnants of chocolate on the tip of her tongue mixing with Curt's own salty flavor. When he removed his fingertip, she automatically licked her lips. Oh, he was very good at this, and she seemed helpless to resist his seductive talents.

The persistent throbbing she'd felt deep within her all day long grew even stronger.

"Isn't it getting late?" she asked in what amounted to a plea. "Maybe we should be heading—"

"And miss our first dance? Heaven forbid."

Before Kathryn could stop him, Curt had pulled her to her feet and was ushering her to the small dance floor in the center of the dining room. "I haven't danced in years," she protested. "I'll probably step all over your toes."

"Go ahead. You're probably as light as a feather."

Curt captured her in his arms and tugged her firmly up against his body, gratified to feel a shudder race through her at the contact. He'd wanted to hold her like this all day. Resisting the urge had been a torturous experience he hadn't expected. She was pretty and inconspicuously alluring on an ordinary day. Now, wearing a lime-green silk dress that clung to her soft curves and flared at her hips, she was truly elegant. But what he'd like best of all would be to hold her in his arms without even the sheerest scrap of fabric between them.

The fact that he knew she responded to him made his need all the more urgent. He could see her desire in the darkening of her eyes, see the rapid rise and fall of her chest as her breathing accelerated whenever he touched her and feel her matching need as she trembled against him. But she was fighting it—like a trooper.

Fortunately Curt enjoyed a challenge. He also liked Kathryn more and more each moment he spent with her. He felt as if he was on the verge of an enormous breakthrough that would finally reveal her secret passions, the real Kathryn Prim she tried so hard to hide.

He slid his hand to the small of her back, moving in rhythm to the music so her pelvis gently discovered his arousal. She sucked in a quick breath and her startled gaze flew up to meet his.

"Curt?"

"Easy, Kate, nothing's going to happen here on the dance floor. You're safe."

"For now," she said with obvious apprehension.

"For as long as you want. Count on it."

"I counted on beating you at tennis, with Stefan's help, and look where it got me."

He guided them out a set of French doors onto a sheltered patio where they could still hear the music. The waves rolling onto the beach provided a subtle counterpoint to the melody. "I admit there are some men you simply can't rely on. Jocks, in particular, are like that."

"Hmm. I'll keep that in mind next time." Lulled by the music, the wine and the warmth of Curt's arms around her, Kathryn rested her head on his shoulder. She liked the feel of his strong body, the press of her breasts against his unyielding chest. It would be so easy to give herself over to the feelings he created. A part of her felt disengaged from reality, floating like a kite suddenly free of its earthly tether.

With a single finger, he lifted her chin and his lips pressed gently against hers. At first the kiss was tentative, like rays of sunlight probing the morning fog along the beach. When there was no resistance, he grew more insistent.

Kathryn tasted wine and chocolate and the sweet flavor of strawberries...and the uniqueness that was Curt. His velvet tongue probed with talented expertise. Unbidden, her hands swept up his broad shoulders and her fingers curled through the fine hair at his nape, threading themselves among the silky brown waves she'd longed to explore.

Her heart pounded like crashing breakers on a rocky shore; her breathing raced like the wind across an open beach.

A throaty sound escaped her and she heard a responding groan.

"Curt, we can't do this," she whispered against his lips.

"Not here. Upstairs." His breathing was as ragged as her own, the press of his arousal urgent and demanding against the sensitive apex of her thighs. "Your place or mine. Name it, Katie. Whatever you say."

She froze. The name he'd called her, the realization that all of his plans led to one single destination, chilled her like an arctic blast. In high school she'd been Katie the Kissable. Hungry for love and affection, she'd flirted outrageously with the boys. Led them on, she admitted. And a couple of times she'd actually believed they cared for her. She'd learned otherwise quickly enough, at the cost of heartache and an already shaky reputation. She'd been the talk of the town, the kind of girl every guy thought he had an absolute right to bed...then brag about later, whether anything had happened or not.

Tears burned at the backs of her eyes. Dear God, she couldn't go through that again.

"No." Her refusal came out a hoarse whisper as she steeled herself against her baser instincts and gritted her teeth. "The date's over. I've paid the wager. In full. Now I want to go home."

"But, Katie—"

"The plane and pilot are still waiting, aren't they?"

"Well, yes, but—"

"Then send the bellboy up to the rooms to get my things, because I'm leaving. On your plane, if you can manage to get it off the ground, or I'm going to hire a taxi to take me all the way back to L.A. and I'll see you get the bill."

She whirled away only to be confronted by an impish woman with a huge camera in her hands.

"Hi, Mr. Creighton," the young woman said. "How 'bout a pic to remember the evening by?"

Kathryn quickly averted her face from the camera. What she didn't need was a photo of her near foolhardiness, or a condemning camera shot that might appear on a grocery-store tabloid for friends and co-workers to see. Or, God help her, a picture her father might see. Her stomach roiled at the very thought.

"Not tonight, Connie," Curt said tersely. He pulled a few bills from his pocket and stuffed them in her camera case. "Maybe next time."

"Thanks, Mr. C."

"No sweat. Take good care of my favorite kids."

Kathryn fled from the open-air terrace before she could hear if the children mentioned were Curt's, or if he simply had an affinity for sexy young women.

DOGGEDLY, CURT FOLLOWED in her footsteps, but she refused to slow down long enough to talk until they were back on the plane. What happened in the next hour or so—his ability to get her to open up and tell him about the pain she was carrying around—was going to make or break their relationship. He knew that. And knew if he handled the situation wrong, he was going to lose somebody special.

Sitting in a swivel chair facing Kathryn, Curt waited to speak until the plane reached cruising altitude and the engines settled into a comfortable hum.

"Tell me what's going on, Katie. All of a sudden you bolted, just when we seemed to be getting along so well."

Her head snapped up and she glared at him. "You mean it was about the time you thought you were going to get into my pants."

"Come on, Katie. You know there's more between us than sex."

"Do I? You've spent weeks trying to seduce me. And you almost succeeded." Kathryn hugged her arms to her stomach to block out the painful realization she had very nearly given in to her desires. "But I'm not sixteen anymore. I've got enough sense not to fall for a guy with a smooth line, and I don't want to be just another conquest some guy can brag about to his buddies in the locker room."

"I'd never..." Confusion leveled his eyebrows. "What are you talking about?"

"I haven't always been *Ms. Prim*, Curt. In fact, twelve years ago, in high school, my reputation was quite the opposite. Katie the Kissable they called me, among other unpleasant nicknames. All of them *earned* and most of them I wouldn't want to repeat in polite company."

"You mean all of this is because some kids in school picked on you?"

"No. It's because I learned to hate being gossiped about. I learned that you can't trust men, and you sure as hell can't trust sex."

He looked more puzzled than shocked by her confession. She'd expected him to react more strongly, perhaps even with revulsion. For so many years she'd kept her past a secret, had created a whole new image for herself, that when a large chunk of the truth had unexpectedly slipped out, she'd anticipated the worst. Instead, Curt had barely blinked.

"That's why you go into your frozen ice-maiden act when I call you Katie?"

"You're a little slow, Creighton, but you're finally catching on."

"My God, are you telling me you've been celibate for *twelve* years? That's got to mean you're scared, Katie, scared of being with a man."

She flushed and trembled at how close he'd come to a truth she didn't want to face. "I'm not afraid. And I've asked you *not* to call me Katie."

"I told you before, sweetheart. When you're with me, the past doesn't matter. If I call you Katie, it's because that's my name for you. Nobody else's. A bunch of punk kids from high school sure as hell don't own it. You're *my* Katie now and you're going to learn to trust me."

She drew on her inner strength, lifted her chin and met his gaze. "Curt, in the past thirteen years I've learned to take responsibility for my actions. Dating you is wrong for me. It can't lead anywhere because I won't allow myself to be connected with a man who attracts gossip like ants are drawn to honey. It simply won't work."

"I won't accept that, Katie. When I'm with you, I feel something powerful is happening between us. You can't throw that away. And I don't intend to give up on us."

"You have to."

Chapter Eight

Rudy whipped the eggs into a froth and, with a flourish, he poured the mixture into an omelet pan. Hot butter sizzled.

"*Très bon!* The omelet, she will lift your spirits," he promised.

Kathryn didn't think a few eggs would do the trick. Resting her elbow on the breakfast counter as she watched Rudy fuss in her kitchen, she rubbed her temple. How could she have been so foolish as to go anywhere with Curt Creighton? She'd barely escaped the *master of seduction* with her good sense intact.

Yesterday at Pebble Beach—last night, in particular—had taught her just how fragile a hold she had on her self-control. A little soft music, a sip or two of wine, a single kiss, and she'd been oh so close to tumbling into bed with Curt Creighton.

God, hadn't she learned anything since she was a teenager?

With a shudder, she pulled the tie of her terry-cloth robe more snugly around her waist.

The shrill sound of the telephone made Kathryn jump. It didn't take a genius to know who was on the other end of the line.

"*Chérie,* do you wish me to answer the phone for you?"

She shook her head.

"But it is the third time he has called in the past hour."

"I know."

He'd started calling at ten that morning. Now it was noon, and this was the sixth time the damn phone had rung. Curt Creighton didn't know the meaning of the word quit.

On the third ring the answering machine switched on.

"Time to rise and shine, Katie my girl," Curt's warm, baritone voice announced. "You can't hide all day. I've been out and bought us a couple of kites. Figured we could go down to Venice Beach to try them out. Whatta ya say?"

He paused but didn't hang up.

Tears pooled in Kathryn's eyes. One damp drop managed to creep over the edge and slip down her cheek in a warm path. For a moment on Pebble Beach she'd been as free as the kite they'd flown together. All too soon, reality had brought her back down to earth.

"Come on. It'd be fun," he cajoled. Then with a trace of stubbornness bordering on desperation, he said, "Damn it, Katie, I care about you. Doesn't that count for something?"

She covered her mouth with her hand to prevent a sob. *Please make him go away before I do something foolish.*

He sighed deeply, conjuring up an image of a man at least temporarily accepting defeat. Then he broke the connection. The answering machine clicked to a stop.

"I think, *chérie,* this is a man who is good for you."

"No," she wailed. "He's all wrong for me. Absolutely wrong." Her chin puckered and her lower lip quivered as if to contradict every word she spoke.

"Ah, yes, now I see how it is with you and this tall, good-looking man who is so insistent." Rudy slid the omelet onto a prewarmed plate and delivered it to Kathryn with the addition of two buttered slices of toast. "It was much the same for me and my sweet Annie . . . Antoinette Bilou. We were wrong for each other, you know? An impossible match. Her parents did not approve. And I had hardly a centime to my name."

To be polite Kathryn cut a bite of the omelet and levered it to her mouth. She had no appetite at all, and she'd agreed to let Rudy fix her a late breakfast only because she lacked the strength to argue with him.

"But none of that mattered," Rudy continued, "because Annie and I loved each other. Just as you, *mon amie,* love this man named Curt."

Her head snapped up. "I don't—"

"Do not deny it, *chérie.* I see your tears and the way your hand trembles, the flush on your cheeks since that first time he came to your door. He brings excitement to your life. Even when you do not answer the phone, your heart waits to hear the sound of his voice. I, too, tried to stay away from my Annie. It only made us both miserable."

"But you did leave her," Kathryn protested. "You came here, to the States, to Hollywood."

"We had a plan." He shrugged. "But it is folly for you to ignore the feelings of your heart. You must accept the truth, *mon amie.* You have fallen in love with the same man you work so hard to avoid."

The fork slid from Kathryn's grasp and clattered onto the plate. She hugged herself, rocking back and forth on the bar stool at the breakfast counter. Rudy had ferreted out her awful secret as easily as if she'd given him a script. She didn't know what had given her away. She'd tried so hard to hide the truth even from herself. Nor did she know the exact instant when her heart had taken over her life from her intellect.

It might have been as early as the day Curt had nearly killed himself at aerobics, or as recently as when he'd taught her to fly a kite. But there it was. Guilty as charged. Dull, stodgy, bookish, boring, *private* Kathryn Prim, who had worked so hard at being just what she was, *loved* Curt Creighton, bachelor millionaire and darling of the tabloids.

It hurt like hell!

IN THE MIDAFTERNOON SUN, Curt lay in a chaise next to the pool, soaking up the rays. A shower of cold water splashed across his chest.

"Geez! What are you doing?"

Pulling up a chair, Lucy plopped herself down next to her big brother. "You look positively morose."

"Tell me about it," Curt grumbled.

"That bad, eh?"

"Worse."

She raised her eyebrows. "I was surprised to find you at home. I figured you'd spend the whole weekend at Pebble Beach."

"I had high hopes," he conceded.

"If it means anything, I like Kathryn."

"So do I."

"Seriously?"

He turned his head and lifted his dark glasses away from his bloodshot eyes. "Yeah. Seriously."

"About time." With a sigh, Lucy leaned back in her chair and propped her feet on a low table. Her shorts were about as short as they came, and her top was downright miniscule. Silver earrings dangled from her ears. "There are days when I wish we were poor."

"Poor? Remember what Mom said. Poor means scratching in the dirt, going hungry and raising the world's worst corn."

"Well, maybe not *that* poor."

Curt laughed, a low, rumbling sound. "You'll find somebody, Sis. You're one terrific lady."

"Thanks." She stared off toward the distant haze of Los Angeles for a few moments and sighed again. "The trouble is, most of the guys I meet are in show business. Which is okay, of course, but sometimes they're a little flaky, and I never know if they're interested only in getting their hands on enough money to produce a colossal box-office flop, or if they really like me. I'd kinda like someone more down to earth. You know, a nice, steady accountant. Or truck driver."

"I'll keep my eyes open."

"I'd appreciate it." She grinned and then her expression grew more serious. "What went wrong between you and Kathryn?"

"She's carrying around a whole lot of hurt."

"You sure you didn't come on too fast? You do have a tendency to do that, you know."

"Maybe," he conceded. "But mostly somebody's laid a whole lot of pain on her."

"When we were kids—after Mom died—you were pretty darn good about kissing my hurts away when I skinned my knees. Rhetorically speaking, I mean. Or rebuilding my shattered ego when some jerk in high school teed me off. Maybe you can do the same for Kathryn."

"Think so?"

"Yeah, I do. In case you didn't know it, big brother, I'm your number-one fan. You'll think of something."

"I hope so." He gave her a wry grin. It was one thing to distract a kid sister when she'd stubbed her toe and make her smile again. Kathryn's revelations had been a whole lot more serious. So far, his ploy of offering a day of flying kites hadn't worked. He'd have to think of something else.

Restless energy drove Curt to his feet.

"Where're you going?" Lucy asked.

"I've got to do some serious thinking."

He made his way to the part of the Creighton property his mother had always referred to as the "back forty." From a toolshed he dragged out a hoe and started hacking at the weeds that had grown nearly waist high. This seemed like a good time to get in touch with his roots. Maybe through osmosis he'd learn something from his mother.

AT NEARLY MIDNIGHT, Curt stood in front of Kathryn's door. He had an urge to lower his shoulder and smash the damn thing in. Instead he leaned a kite against the doorjamb. She'd find it in the morning. Maybe then she'd get his message.

He wasn't real good at accepting rejection. Lack of experience, he supposed.

Tugging his motorcycle helmet back on, he wondered what his dad had finally done to win his mother. Curt wished he'd asked when he had the chance.

LYING SLEEPLESS in her bed, Kathryn heard the sound of the departing motorcycle, just as she'd heard its arrival.

When the engine noise faded into the sounds of distant traffic on the boulevard, she got up.

Making her way in the dark, for fear Curt had circled back and was parked somewhere nearby waiting to spot her telltale light, she walked from the bedroom through the living room. Cautiously she opened the front door. In the dim glow from the hallway fixtures, she saw the beautiful butterfly kite decorated in bright shades of a rainbow.

She lifted it into her arms as though it were the most precious artwork in the world. This gift, she vowed, would be the one she kept. A memory to cling to in the empty years ahead.

"I IMAGINE *you* had a really nice weekend," the smiling receptionist drawled by way of greeting the next morning.

"It was fine, thank you," Kathryn responded levelly. *Fine* if you didn't mind going sleepless for two nights and feeling as if you'd been dragged through the worst final exam of your life.

She walked through the plushly furnished law-office lobby, down the hallway and into the small lunchroom where a never-empty coffeepot beckoned. Heavy doses of caffeine might keep her going through the day.

"My gracious, Kathryn!" gushed Evelyn Hall, one of the secretaries. "Aren't you just the one? Nobody even guessed. And I'm *sooo* envious."

Kathryn's jaw went slack and her hand rested immobile on the coffeepot handle as Evelyn breezed out of the room. Envious of what? she wondered.

With a puzzled shake of her head, Kathryn poured herself the cup of coffee she'd been after.

She'd nearly made it to her office when Julia passed her in the aisle.

"Good for you, hon," Julia whispered conspiratorially. "Go for it! Big time!" The young woman giggled, then hurried toward the cubicle where she made magic happen with a computer.

A frown tugged at Kathryn's forehead. Something was definitely going on here. Something not quite right. It had the uncomfortable feel of Curt Creighton and Seduction Incorporated.

She drew in a breath, gritted her teeth and stepped into her office.

A surprisingly sharp surge of disappointment washed over her when she discovered no room full of roses, no colorful kites dangling from the ceiling, no extravagant gifts piled on her desk. In fact, the only object out of place in her orderly office was a tabloid newspaper resting smack in the middle of her otherwise neat and tidy desk. A tabloid newspaper featuring a collage of photos, she realized with growing horror. Pictures of playboy millionaire Curt Creighton with his latest *lover,* the headline shrieked.

Kathryn's knees buckled and she sank into her chair. Her worst nightmare...

In every pose, the photographer had caught them at what could easily be construed as a suggestive moment. In the tennis-court scene captured by the photographer, Curt's hand looped provocatively behind Kathryn's head, his face close to hers, as though they were about to kiss. Curt held her even more intimately while they danced at Pebble Beach, his hand splayed across the swell of her rear. Somehow the photographer had even managed to make the sweet memory of their flying kites together dirty and lurid.

The article itself implied a weekend of lewd, lascivious behavior at an undisclosed location. There weren't any facts. Only implication. Innuendo. Gossip of the very worst sort.

Her hands shook and the newspaper trembled. God, she didn't deserve that kind of distortion of the truth. Not again. Not like the whole town of Waverly had done to her as a teenager. This time the whole *world* would believe the lies.

"Katie?"

At the soft call of her name, she turned and looked up into Curt's blue-green eyes, eyes that looked as weary as Kathryn felt. She fought both the way her chin quivered and an urge to fly into his arms.

"I'm so sorry, Katie. I came as soon as I heard about the damn story. I swear I didn't know the paparazzi had followed us to Pebble Beach. I never meant for that to happen."

"How...how do you stand it? All those lies? Everything you do, you do in a fishbowl. Helicopters hovering over your house to get a juicy shot. People peering at you through huge lenses and hiding behind trees when you go to the beach."

He lifted his shoulders in an uneasy shrug. His leather jacket hung open and his shirttail wasn't tucked in, as though he had dressed hurriedly—or had slept in his clothes. "Most of the time it doesn't matter. I don't care what they say about me. Except once when some cretin accused me of having ties to the mob. That really bugged me. As for the women I usually date, they figure any publicity is good publicity. Career enhancement."

"I hate it."

"They're only words written on a piece of paper," he stressed. "They can't hurt you."

"Oh, yes, they can. They can make people think the worst. They're lies."

"Your friends won't believe that junk and no one else is important. Beyond the fact that nothing actually happened, we're two consenting adults. No one's going to object."

"I do. I hate being talked about."

"I understand that now. If I could, I'd take back every damn copy of that paper and burn them all. But I can't do that."

She stood and drew herself to her full five feet five inches, lifting her chin in her most professional manner, all the while thinking surely her heart would break. "Then you can certainly understand why I don't wish to see you again."

Without flinching, she withstood his scrutiny as the seconds ticked by one after the other. She noted and filed in her memory the way his gaze swept over her, lingering far too long on the rise and fall of her breasts, his burning look sending her thoughts into forbidden directions. The determined look in his eyes penetrated the barriers she had erected as though he were aware of every heated thought she desperately tried to suppress.

"You sure that's how you want it?" he asked.

In a moment of instinctive denial, she shook her head. "I want you to stay away," she lied to cover her mental lapse. What she really wanted was for Curt to be an absolute *nobody* who wouldn't even make it into the obituary column when he died of old age. She wanted anonymity. She wanted to hide— and Curt lived on the front page.

To her dismay, he'd seen her lapse for what it was—the truth.

With the swiftness of a true predator, Curt slipped the rest of the way into her office and closed the door behind him. Before Kathryn could object he gathered her in his arms. His lips crossed hers, first at one enticing angle, and then shifting to another. His tongue slid between her lips as if it had every right to be there, and he plundered the tender flesh that remembered so well his velvety touch, his sweet, rich taste.

Kathryn's clenched fists pressed in sweet frustration against his unyielding chest. Slowly, as Curt persisted, her fingers relaxed, her body refusing to fight his erotic onslaught a moment longer. The kiss went on and on, draining her resistance and taking her breath away. His talented fingers found their way under her blouse, eager to explore her silk undergarments. With easy precision, he located and cupped her breast with his palm, using his thumb to stimulate her nipple into a hard, aching nub.

Vaguely, over the sound of her rapid breathing, she heard people chatting in the hallway and the rumble of the copy machine in the next office. The inappropriateness of what they were doing—the sinfully dangerous act of carrying on in her office when anyone might step through the unlocked door unannounced—aroused Kathryn to a frenzy of excitement.

Dear God, she wanted Curt to strip her naked and take her right there on top of her desk. She wanted to wrap her legs around his waist, feel him fill her and damn all the rules, all the shocked expressions, all the restrictions of polite society. He'd done this awful thing to her, turned her into a wanton who could think only of sweaty bodies twisting and writhing together. Hers. His. On the desk. On the floor. It really didn't matter. She wanted it all. Now.

"Please," she whispered in a hoarse plea against his lips.

His breathing as ragged as her own, Curt framed her face with his big, rough hands. "You want to try telling me again you don't want to see me?"

She swallowed hard. How could she make a claim like that when the opposite was so desperately obvious? She gave an almost imperceptible shake of her head.

"There aren't going to be any more lies between us, Katie. Most of all, I'm not going to let you lie to yourself ever again, and you're going to stop punishing yourself for what happened years ago."

"You don't play fair, Creighton," she complained.

Disarming dimples creased both of his cheeks. "You're damn right, sweetheart."

Chapter Nine

Briefcase in hand, Kathryn wove her way through the crowded courthouse corridor. By pleading a combination of homework and fatigue, she'd managed to avoid Curt for the past couple of days, since the publication of that awful tabloid feature. She'd also gotten up enough nerve to call her sister again, taking the easy way out and phoning during the day to avoid contact with her father. Soon she was going to have to face her past. She knew she wouldn't be able to move forward with her life until she did.

For now, however, Curt was the person she had to face. The case of *Kellogg v. Creighton* had her trapped. She had to be in court, even though other deadlines had kept her away while jury selection proceeded. Tom Weston insisted he needed her now. Of course, Curt would be there, too. Any minute.

She slanted a glance at Ms. Kellogg, who stood beside her attorney in the trash-littered hallway. They had her dressed like a sweet little girl right off the farm in a drab beige outfit, and she'd colored her hair a shade of brown that was almost as lifeless. An old ploy, Kathryn mused, but one that didn't quite work when Roz tossed her hair over her shoulder in a naturally seductive gesture, or swayed her hips provocatively as she walked.

The neck brace was a nice touch, too. Kathryn smiled as she pictured passionate lovemaking so athletic as to cause a whiplash injury that lasted for weeks. Certainly a night to remember... but hardly credible in a court of law.

Did they really think the jury would believe the mousy woman her attorneys were trying to portray? Or the poorly disguised sexpot underneath?

Kathryn gritted her teeth and fought off a raging case of jealousy. She didn't want to believe anything about Roslyn Kellogg's story. And she hoped the plaintiff's attorney hadn't been smart enough to get a photo of the condemning circular bed with the matching overhead mirror.

In contrast to Roslyn's pathetic effort at deception, Curt's appearance as he strode down the hallway fairly shouted wealth and sophistication—hand-tailored suit, expensive silk tie and Italian shoes that gleamed. But it was the smile he meant just for Kathryn that took her breath away. Until that moment she hadn't actually realized her heart could do a flip-flop. Quite an extraordinary sensation, one she gamely tried to control.

At Curt's side, his sister, Lucy, sailed along oblivious to reporters trying to mob them and the frequent snap of flashbulbs. Her dangling earrings threw the light back at the photographers in starbursts of energy.

Curt gave Kathryn a long, appreciative look, then shifted his attention to Tom, extending his hand in greeting. At the same time, Lucy gave Kathryn a quick hug, whispering, "All you have to do is keep playing hard to get, just like you've been doing, and Curt will be on his knees. Good job."

"That's not what—" Kathryn objected, but Lucy had already turned toward Tom.

"I don't think you've met my sister," Curt said to the lawyer. "Lucy, meet the best attorney in town, Tom Weston."

"My goodness, big brother, you didn't tell me he's also the *best-looking* attorney in town." She looked him up and down as if he was a winning contestant in the Mr. Universe contest.

A blush rose up Tom's neck and colored his cheeks. Kathryn felt a rush of sympathy for her boss. He was such a reserved individual in terms of personal relationships, she doubted he'd ever been looked at in quite that way.

Tom cleared his throat. "I'm pleased to meet you, Ms. Creighton."

"Please call me Lucy, honey. Everyone does." She hooked her arm through Tom's. "Let's get away from all these praying mantises from the press, and you can tell me all about the strategy you're going to use to whip the panty hose off sweet little Roz. I just know you've thought of something wonderful. Maybe a trick that's just a tiny bit vindictive?" she asked hopefully as she swept Tom into the courtroom. "I hate that I misjudged that woman."

Kathryn met Curt's amused gaze with one of her own. "Your sister isn't exactly bashful," she remarked.

"Family trait. We Creightons are a self-assured bunch."

"So I've noticed."

"The object is to keep the other guy—or gal—off balance. Like now, when I tell you how much I want to kiss you right here in front of everybody."

Her eyes widened. "Don't you dare!" she warned in a hoarse whisper.

"Oh, I won't act on the impulse," he agreed in a low, sultry voice meant only for her. "But that won't stop me from thinking about the warmth of your lips, your special flavor, the texture of your tongue brushing against mine, the way your pulse beats—"

Face flaming hot, Kathryn whirled and pushed through the courtroom doors. Curt's teasing chuckle followed her into the room. Lord, with only a few words, Curt had the power to increase her heart rate higher than a good aerobics session. And the worst part was that he had articulated precisely what she'd been thinking.

Taking her place next to Tom at the defendant's table, as far away as possible from where Curt would sit, Kathryn flipped open her briefcase. Her hands shook. Maybe Lucy was right. Kathryn had been playing so hard to get, Curt thought of her as a challenge. Perhaps if she stopped running away, he would lose interest and move on to the next woman who happened to cross his path, leaving Kathryn alone.

On that thoroughly depressing note, she turned to scan the courtroom.

Roz, her attorney and a second man were hurrying down the aisle. While Roz and her attorney took their places at the plaintiff's table, the other man found a seat in the front row right behind them. Dressed in a polyester suit and wearing a garish tie, he looked like a two-bit hood who split his time between pushing drugs and pimping.

Shuddering at the thought, Kathryn leaned forward so she could question Curt.

"Is the man sitting behind Roz her boyfriend?" she asked.

Curt glanced over his shoulder. "Yeah, that's him."

"What does he do for a living?"

"No visible means of support that I know about," Curt replied.

"You know his name?"

"Walter...Walter Simms, I think."

Kathryn jotted a note on her yellow legal pad.

"Are you on to something?" Tom asked in a low voice.

"I don't know," she confessed. "I'm picking up bad vibes from this Simms fellow. It's probably nothing. Maybe just his lousy taste in ties."

"Trust your instincts, Kathryn. Sometimes that's better than a year's worth of law school."

The judge entered, a tall, angular black woman with a reputation that matched her unforgiving scowl. "Let's get under way," she ordered brusquely, rapping her gavel for order. The jury settled into their seats in the jury box, focusing their attention on the opposing attorneys.

Kathryn took notes and listened for inconsistencies while the plaintiff's doctor described Ms. Kellogg's injuries that had resulted from the evening in question. Considering she'd fallen no more than three feet, Roz had certainly suffered a lot of bruises to go with a strained back and her fake whiplash, Kathryn mused. It sounded more as though she'd been *thrown* out of bed, rather than simply toppled over the side.

As usual, Tom did a good job challenging the doctor's credibility, forcing the man to admit that nearly ninety percent of his patients were accident victims. The guy was a real ambulance chaser.

The plaintiff's attorney then called LaVerne Raddison. Wearing a tailored suit, the young woman looked sophisticated and very capable as she made her way to the witness box. Not at all like her usual effervescent self.

"When you heard the cries of alarm, what did you do?" the attorney asked after he had established LaVerne had been present at the Creighton home the night of the accident.

"I went running into Roz's room."

"And what did you discover there?"

"Roz was on the floor next to the bed."

"And Mr. Creighton?"

"He was there, too. Trying to help her up."

"What were Mr. Creighton and Ms. Kellogg wearing when you observed this?"

LaVerne shot Curt a troubled look. "Nothing," she said softly.

"I'm sorry, miss," the attorney said. "I don't think the jury heard your response. Would you tell us again, please? How were the couple dressed when you found them?"

"They weren't a couple, Mr.—"

"Just answer my question," the attorney persisted.

LaVerne hesitated and pulled her lower lip between her teeth. "They were both naked."

"As if they had been making love?"

Kathryn's entire body clenched in denial at the possibility that Curt had ever made love to Roz. Surely not.

"Objection!" Tom shouted. "Calls for conjecture on the part of the witness."

"Sustained," the judge ruled.

Kathryn breathed a sigh of relief when Tom had a chance to question LaVerne and undo the damage she had done. She seemed so totally sincere about her relationship with Curt, and that of the other women who stayed at the mansion, she was a far better witness for the defense than the plaintiff. At least, Kathryn hoped that was the case. As flighty as LaVerne and her twin could be, Kathryn was actually beginning to like the two young women.

In retaliation, the plaintiff's attorney tried to discredit LaVerne's testimony, accusing her of practically being on the Creighton payroll.

And so it went—fence and parry—for most of the morning.

When Roz took the stand in her own behalf, Kathryn found herself leaning forward as if by getting an inch or two closer she could intimidate the plaintiff into telling the truth. Curt had never made love to her. *Go ahead, admit it,* Kathryn mentally urged the well-rehearsed plaintiff. The woman was a little too smooth, whereas most witnesses show at least some signs of nerves when they testify. A damn good actress, Kathryn concluded.

Kathryn's continued intense study of Roslyn revealed a slight discoloration on Roz's jaw only partially hidden by her makeup. And as she looked more closely, Kathryn discovered a similar bruise on Roz's upper arm. This lady either bruised easily or she was getting boxed around, probably by the sleazy guy who had escorted her into the courtroom.

Kathryn jotted down her suspicions and slipped Tom the note.

Another thought occurred to Kathryn as Roz continued her testimony. Curt's incredible wealth made him vulnerable to more than frivolous lawsuits. He'd be at the mercy of greedy women who wanted a chunk of his money more than they cared about Curt as a man.

She stole a peek at Curt. What cruel irony that she would have preferred him to be an honest, but poor, motorcycle-riding messenger rather than a much-touted bachelor millionaire.

Only a muscle rippling at his jaw gave away the tension Curt was experiencing. He was a man used to hiding his feelings, Kathryn realized—most often behind an easy grin. She'd begun to suspect the real Curt Creighton had more depth than he bothered to let on. She wondered why.

Curt shifted uneasily in his chair. He knew he was sweating. It wasn't so much what Roz was saying. Hell, he'd heard and read worse slander about himself. He simply hated that Kathryn had to hear the lies.

In the past he'd always been of the words-could-never-hurt-him philosophy and there wasn't much he could do about what others thought of him, anyway.

With Kathryn it was different. He cared. A lot. And he hated that there was no way he could stop the perjurious testimony.

AT LAST THE JUDGE called for a lunch break.

"What a dreadful woman!" Lucy was standing in front of Tom before he had a chance to gather up all of his papers. "What you need, my dears—all three of you, of course—is a quiet, relaxing lunch. I've arranged everything. Martinelli's deli has delivered it all to Judge Wilcox's chambers."

"Judge W. Wilcox?" Tom stammered. "The presiding judge?" A man who Kathryn knew thought of himself as no lower than the left hand of God…and sometimes a notch or two above that.

"He's an old friend of the family and is delighted to have us use his conference room."

"I don't really think we should—"

"Nonsense, Thomas." Lucy scooped up the rest of Tom's papers, shoved them haphazardly into the briefcase and firmly snapped it shut. "Martinelli's pastrami is out of this world. And his half-dill pickles. Mmmm…" She kissed her fingertips in a flamboyantly seductive gesture. "You'll love it all."

Curt clamped his hand on the back of Tom's blushing neck in a thoroughly macho way. "Come on, old man. I promise to protect you from my overeager sis—"

"I'm not!" she protested.

"And we'll have a chance," Curt continued, "to avoid the press that's sure to be waiting outside that door. Including about ten thousand photographers."

Kathryn thought avoiding those jerks with the cameras was the best idea she'd heard all day. "He's right, Tom. It'll be quiet in the judge's chambers, and there won't be any interruptions while you go over Curt's testimony."

Tom's reluctance to be led by Lucy into the judge's chambers was as amusing as it was surprising. Kathryn had never seen him quite so off balance. But then the Creighton siblings seemed to have that effect on everyone they met.

Curt slid into a chair at the end of the conference table and accepted a pastrami sandwich from his sister. The two things he hated most in life were liars and greedy people. Roz Kellogg represented the worst of both. It all seemed so unnecessary, particularly since Lucy had told him Roz had enough talent to make it as an actress. Pity she'd wasted it on a frivolous lawsuit and one big scene in the courtroom. When she lost—and Curt was pretty confident she would—the press would drag the poor woman's reputation through the mud. She wouldn't even be able to get a job as an extra.

A terrible waste of her talents.

Kathryn, on the other hand, made the most of her abilities, he mused. He could tell by the way she followed the testimony so alertly that not much would get past her. Smart lady.

His admiration for her clicked up another notch.

THE REMAINING TWO DAYS of the trial went on in pretty much the same fashion—testimony supporting each side, character witnesses, pictures of that awful bed that made Kathryn cringe. During each recess, Lucy managed to take over, soothing and reassuring Tom at every opportunity that he couldn't possibly lose the case. Kathryn tended to agree.

The following evening, as Kathryn was letting herself into her apartment after her night class, she heard the phone ringing. Picking up the phone, she smiled in anticipation of what had become a chaste but strangely titillating evening ritual.

"About time you got home" came Curt's sexy, teasing voice. "I've missed you."

"Professor Adkins found the case of *Smithers v. New Jersey* particularly engrossing."

"How 'bout you?"

"Fascinating," she lied, shrugging out of her jacket. She'd hardly heard a word the instructor had said. Instead, she'd been thinking about Curt—how he'd looked in court that day, and what they would talk about tonight.

"I'm envious."

"Why's that?"

"I don't like the thought of any man besides me holding your attention."

"Would it ease your mind if I told you he was eighty-two years old?"

"Is he?"

"No."

The sound of his rich, mellow laughter warmed a spot right next to Kathryn's heart, a place that had been cold for a long time without her even realizing it.

"Ah, sweet Katie, you make it hard for a guy to keep up with you, but I'm not going to stop trying."

She squeezed the phone hard as a band of emotion tightened around her chest. Lord help her, she was beginning to like the way he said her name. *Katie.* From his lips it sounded like adulation.

They talked a while longer, then as the hour grew late he proceeded to tell her what he'd like to do if she were willing. Secret, intimate things that made her ache for him. Wonderfully erotic acts she'd never even dreamed about.

As he spoke she had to remind herself that Curt Creighton's photo would land on the front page of the morning newspaper with twenty inches of column space devoted to his rather colorful private life. A similar story had appeared in every edition since the trial began. That was the kind of media attention he attracted—the kind of attention she abhorred.

Darn it all! She was falling in love with the one man who should have been at the very bottom of her list.

"It's late, Curt. I've got to go."

"Sure, sweetheart. You'll be in court tomorrow?"

"Yes," she whispered, tortured by the thought that she didn't dare fall in love with this particular man and yet she couldn't seem to stop herself.

CURT HUNG UP THE PHONE and checked his watch. Well after midnight. He wasn't in the least bit tired. Talking to Katie made him feel exactly the opposite. Wired!

The lady was weakening. He could hear it in the breathless sound of her voice and see it in the darkening of her eyes each time they met in court.

But damn if he wasn't going to have to speak to the staff of the Seduction Incorporated catalog. They could all get sued for misleading advertising. Silks, diamonds and Cadillacs didn't have a prayer of working with Kathryn.

She liked soft talk and flying kites.

He liked that in a woman. He liked that a whole lot.

"HAVE YOU REACHED a verdict?" the judge asked the jury foreman when the court was called back into session midafternoon.

"We have, your honor."

"Well, let's not keep it a secret." Still wearing her perpetual scowl, the judge read the verdict as delivered by the bailiff, then handed it back.

The foreman cleared his throat, then said, "We find for the defendant, your honor."

The judge banged the gavel in a futile effort to quell the swelling buzz of conversation in the courtroom. "The jury's dismissed, with our thanks. Court is adjourned."

Muscles in Kathryn's neck and shoulders that she had held bunched up for days finally eased their tight grip on her nerves. She blew out a relieved sigh. The jury didn't think Curt was guilty of anything, at least not where Roz was concerned. Neither did she. With his wealth, he was simply an easy target for people with more greed than good sense.

She slanted a curious glance in the direction of Walter Simms. He didn't look like a man content with the jury's decision, and his hostile expression made Kathryn's skin crawl.

But then Curt was on his feet, blocking her view of Simms while shaking hands with Tom. An instant later Lucy was right there, too, giving the attorney a hug and a kiss that lingered long enough to suggest the two of them had been spending time on their own getting acquainted.

"I'd kiss you, too," Curt said privately as he took Kathryn's hand in a professional handshake, "but the press is everywhere. The two of us in a clench would be sure to make the front page. We'll let Lucy have the attention this time around."

"Thank you," she whispered. Emotion filled her chest and she could have kissed him for his thoughtfulness, his willingness to save her from embarrassment.

"Fact is, Lucy has planned a celebration party for us. A quiet dinner for four at a place that bars the paparazzi. Will you come?"

"I'm not sure that's wise."

"Lucy won't take no for an answer. She's like a steamroller when she gets her mind set on something."

"I gathered as much. I've even considered warning Tom, but I think it's too late."

He gave her one of those irresistible grins. "I'll pick you up at seven."

Before she allowed herself to fully consider the consequences, Kathryn nodded her agreement. "At seven."

Even as the press corps flowed around and past her in their pursuit of Curt and his sister, Kathryn wondered at her decision. If she didn't stay away from Curt, how could she possibly keep her heart intact? Because with each strobe of a flashbulb it grew increasingly clear that his life-style starkly contrasted with what she could tolerate.

In grateful anonymity, she slipped out of the courthouse, found her car and crept through heavy traffic back to her apartment. Rudy intercepted Kathryn before she could get her key in the door lock.

"Ah, my little chickadee, it seems this man of yours is an innocent, after all."

She laughed. "I'm not sure that's quite how I'd describe him. More likely, the jury figured Curt to be such a good lover he'd never lose a woman over the side of his bed."

"Yes, that is quite likely, but nonetheless you did win the case."

"My boss did. Mostly I did the research on case law. All very boring stuff." She shoved open the door. "Come on in. I'll fix us a cup of tea to celebrate, anyway."

"No, no, *chérie.* Do not go to such bother. I only wished to congratulate you when I heard the news on the television."

Taking Rudy's arm, she urged him through the door. He was looking particularly gaunt, she noticed, a little more stooped than usual and drawn around the mouth. "You're practically family, Rudy. Who better to help me celebrate?" He'd been both neighbor and friend for the past ten years, and more times than not, a surrogate grandfather.

He shuffled into the living room and eased himself into a chair by the window. "I think maybe that young man should be the one who lifts a glass of wine in your honor, not an old fool like me with a cup of tea."

"He's coming for me later," she admitted. Her cheeks grew warm with a blush, but she ignored the sensation. Rudy was too perceptive by far to accept a lie.

"Then I should leave so you may make yourself even more beautiful than usual."

"We'll have tea." She placed her briefcase on an end table, shrugged out of her suit jacket and headed for the kitchen. She didn't like the look of Rudy. Normally he radiated energy like a bouncing ball at the end of a rubber band. "Are you feeling all right?" she asked over her shoulder. "You look a little tired."

"It is nothing. Only a weariness that comes with old age."

Twice he'd mentioned his age. As a rule, Rudy seemed convinced he'd never had a birthday past his fortieth, ready to go the distance with any man half his age. Or any woman, for that matter.

Kathryn fixed Rudy an aromatic herbal tea and watched with concern as he barely sipped the brew.

With shaking hands, he set the cup and saucer on the table. "And now, *mon amie,* I must go so you can ready yourself for your gentleman friend."

"Are you sure you're all right? Maybe you should see a doctor."

He shook his head, then brushed a kiss against her cheek. "You must have a very good time this night with your handsome lover who makes your cheeks glow. A chance lost is one you may never have again."

With those troubling words, he left the apartment. Kathryn might have followed him except she didn't have time to dawdle if she was going to be ready when Curt came to pick her up.

Her wardrobe offered few dressy choices, so after a quick shower she picked the lime-green dress she'd worn in Pebble Beach. Lifting the gown from the hanger, memories swept over her—of the way she had danced with Curt and the evidence of his desire as he held her in his embrace, of the sweet, lingering taste of his kiss. Tonight she would face a new set of challenges. All of them temptingly erotic.

She might have helped win a legal case today, but she didn't for a moment believe she could beat Curt Creighton at his favorite game of seduction. Not any longer. He was simply too masterful a player. His finely honed skills were a work of art.

A few minutes before seven she heard a knock at the door. Smiling, Kathryn decided Curt was as eager as she to explore where this night might lead.

Without checking the peephole, she pulled open the door.

"Rudy?" she questioned, anxiety flaring in her midsection.

"*Chérie.* I think..." Her neighbor's eyes rolled upward, his knees buckled and he collapsed in a boneless heap across her threshold.

Chapter Ten

Fear as sharp as daggers twisted through Curt's gut when he turned the corner onto Kathryn's street. Pulling up to the curb across from her apartment, he parked his Ferrari and leaped out of the car. The revolving ambulance light flicked past him like a bloodred blade.

"Not Katie," he mumbled, dodging a passing car as he ran across the street. "Don't let anything happen to Katie."

He shoved his way through the crowd of gawking onlookers. Rationally, he knew there were at least twenty units in Kathryn's apartment house. He'd seen her only three hours ago and she'd been fine. The chances that something had happened to Kathryn were slim to none. No sensible man would worry about odds like that.

But not a single logical argument reduced the terror that gripped him.

He raced into the building and took the stairs three at a time. The sight of Kathryn's open doorway and the curious neighbors standing around outside her apartment nearly undid him. He burst into the room.

"Hey, fella, you gotta clear the area," a paramedic gruffly ordered.

"Where is she? Where the hell is Kathryn?"

At the sound of Curt's voice, Kathryn whirled around. "Thank heavens you're here," she cried.

An instant after he spotted her looking helpless and frightened in the middle of the room, Curt had her wrapped in his arms, swearing to himself he was never going to let her go. Not ever. Moisture stung at the backs of his eyes. This woman had given him more grief since he'd met her than any other woman had in his entire life.

"My God, Katie, I saw the ambulance and thought something had happened to you. I was so damn scared." He hugged her even tighter as though to emphasize his words. "So scared."

"I'm all right." His concern for her safety, along with the strength of his arms, cocooned Kathryn like a child's fleecy security blanket. She relished the unfamiliar sensation. "It's Rudy. They think he's had a heart attack. I saw him earlier this afternoon and he seemed tired. I gave him some tea but he didn't drink it," she rambled on. "I should have known something was wrong. And then he showed up at my door." Close to hysteria, she gulped for air.

"Shh, love. The paramedics are here. They'll take good care of him."

"He's been like a grandfather to me all these years, Curt. I love him and I don't think I ever told him so."

"Don't worry, sweetheart. He knows. Based on the stunts he's played on me—pretending to be a woman, and then calling me up as if he were Tom— I figure he loves you, too."

She slipped her arms around Curt's middle and rested her head on his chest, accepting his reassurances and watching as the paramedics worked over Rudy. Dear God, it felt good to have someone to lean on. Playboy or not, at the moment he felt rock solid, a man a woman could count on.

The paramedics worked with appalling intensity, applying an oxygen mask, starting an IV. Finally they strapped Rudy onto a stretcher.

"I'm going with him," she announced.

"Which hospital?" Curt asked the ambulance attendant.

"Marina."

"Okay, sweetheart. You ride with Rudy and I'll meet you there."

Grateful for his understanding, she palmed Curt's cheek. "Thank you," she whispered. "I'm sorry about the celebration party."

"Don't be. Rudy comes first. Lucy and Tom will do fine on their own."

SOME TWENTY HOURS LATER Kathryn idly wondered if hospitals intentionally purchased the most uncomfortable furniture they could find for their waiting rooms. To keep out the riffraff, she imagined.

Stretching, she rolled her neck and shifted her shoulders, then gave Curt a weary smile as he handed her another cup of vending machine coffee and a wrapped sandwich.

"You should go home and get some sleep, Katie." He sat down beside her on the rock-hard upholstered bench and began massaging her neck with his thumbs and fingers. "I'll make sure they call you if there's any change in Rudy's condition."

"I can't go until I know he's going to be all right. But you don't have to stay."

"Why is it you're always trying to get rid of me, Ms. Prim?"

"At the moment, I can't think how I would have gotten along without you through all of this." He'd been the calm at the center of her emotional storm, a pillar to lean on. She couldn't remember the last time she'd had someone to rely on besides herself. Perhaps that's what she'd begun to sense in Curt—a man who would be there when you needed him. A staunchly supportive friend under the most difficult of circumstances. Given her adolescent experiences with both boys of her own age and her father, it seemed almost too good to be true.

"But you need your rest, too," she insisted.

"I'm here for the duration, Katie. Count on it."

Willingly, she leaned into the soothing movement of his talented fingers. "If I didn't know better, I'd begin to think you're a really nice guy."

"At last. A woman who appreciates my finer qualities."

"If you didn't make such a point of hiding them behind that playboy image of yours, maybe somebody else would have noticed."

"Hmm. Maybe you're the only one who brings out the best in me."

She shifted so she could see him better. In spite of the fact that his tie was askew, his white shirt collar open and his jacket had long since been tossed aside, he looked considerably better than she felt. In fact, the rumpled look of his wavy hair and the roughness of his beard made him even more desirable than usual. As if that were possible. She imagined she could see Curt morning, noon and night for the rest of her life and find him more appealing each time. The guy certainly had a way of growing on a girl.

The door to the cardiac-care unit swung open. Kathryn was on her feet almost before the doctor—garbed in hospital greens—could speak.

"Mr. Franco is awake now, Ms. Prim. You can see him but only for a few minutes. Then I want him to get some rest."

"How is he, Doctor?"

"He's not in any immediate danger. But he's not a young man. I have to be honest with you—we're lucky he's still with us. He had another attack shortly after he arrived in emergency. He's stabilized now, but his system has experienced a great deal of stress. We'll just have to keep our fingers crossed. The eventual outcome may depend on how much he wants to live."

She swallowed hard. "Thank you, Doctor."

Without Curt's reassuring hand on her shoulder, Kathryn might not have made it down the hallway to Rudy's room. His presence gave strength to knees that felt strangely rubbery.

Above the stark hospital bed, the jagged green line on the monitor moved with reassuring regularity across the screen. Assorted tubes snaked from life-giving sources to the frail man who lay there.

Rudy's eyes blinked open when she took his hand. "Ah, *chérie,* I see I have frightened you, no?"

"You have frightened me, yes." She bent over to kiss his forehead. "You're going to have to get well, you know. I couldn't possibly break in a new neighbor."

"Do not worry so, my little chickadee. I am an old man." His eyes looked glassy and slightly out of focus, but his voice was strong. "If I should die, my only regret would be that I would never again see my Antoinette...my Annie. Such a beauty she was, and I such a fool to leave her."

She swallowed hard, remembering how her neighbor had spoken so often about his true love, the woman he had lost. "When you get well, Rudy, we'll go to Paris together,'' Kathryn recklessly promised. ''How does that sound?''

''Ah, to see her again.'' His weak smile brought tears to Kathryn's eyes. ''That is my dream. My life would be complete.'' His voice drifted off and his eyes closed.

A moment later the nurse announced it was time to leave.

Kathryn kissed him one last time and gave his hand another squeeze. ''I love you, my old friend. Be well,'' she whispered.

Opening his eyes, Rudy nodded and looked past her shoulder to Curt. ''You must take care of my little chickadee. She needs a good man in her life.''

''Hush, Rudy,'' she admonished, blushing. ''This is not the time to be matchmaking.''

''I'll do my best,'' Curt assured Rudy, resting his hand momentarily on the older man's shoulder.

In the hallway, Kathryn stopped to take a deep breath. Her emotions felt raw. She fought an overpowering sense of grief. Rudy wasn't dead yet, she reminded herself. She desperately needed to find a way to make Rudy want to live. There were so few people in her life whom she felt free to love.

Curt pulled her into his arms. ''Do you know how to find this Antoinette person Rudy's talking about?'' he asked.

''I have the key to his apartment and I know where his address book is. After he came to the States, she married someone else. She's a widow now and they've corresponded a couple of times. I imagine she's listed in his book—Antoinette Bilou."

"Great. Then let's go get her and bring her back to Rudy."

Resting her head against his chest, she frowned. "You mean phone her and tell her to hop on a plane."

"Not exactly. My idea is to make her travel as comfortable as possible and not have her crammed onto some overbooked airplane, assuming she could even get a flight right away. We'll go pick her up instead."

Kathryn's head snapped up and her jaw went slack. "Go to Paris? Now? I don't even have a passport."

That stopped him but not for long. "Don't worry about it. I've got a friend in the State Department."

"Curt, some functionary in the State Department can't simply whip out a passport on no notice. There are procedures, approvals to get, background checks—"

"Honey, trust me on this. This guy is an old crony of my father. He owes me for a little job I did over in Hong Kong that helped keep things cool a couple of years ago. Besides that, he's tight with the president of France. We'll manage. I'll tell him it's an emergency."

Kathryn looked at him in amazement. Apparently Curt had contacts all over the world—at the highest levels. She truly didn't doubt for a minute he could get her into any country he wanted to—and do it with little more than a phone call.

"My crew keeps the plane fueled and ready," he continued, glancing at his Rolex. "We'd get to Paris by tomorrow afternoon local time, give the crew a few hours to rest and then we could be on our way home again with a surprise for Rudy. If Antoinette can't pump up his spirits, I don't know who can." Curt wore the confident grin Kathryn loved but couldn't quite buy.

"Assuming I don't get jailed for illegal entry...*and* we can actually find Antoinette, what makes you so sure she'd get on a plane with you?"

"Because you'll be with me, and you, my sweet Katie, have an honest face."

She rolled her eyes. "You're crazy, Creighton. Really crazy."

"Definitely one of my more interesting characteristics."

"I can't simply pack up and leave. I have responsibilities. There'd be talk—"

"It's practically the weekend. If we push it, you'll be home in time for work Monday morning and no one except Rudy will be the wiser."

"I don't know..." she hedged. "You talk like whipping over to France is as easy as running down to the grocery store for a loaf of bread."

"It is when you've got your own plane. Let's get you home, so you can pack a change of clothes and a nightie."

"Nightie?" she questioned, raising her eyebrows. "This trip *is* for Rudy's benefit, isn't it?"

With a suspiciously confident grin, he took her elbow and ushered her down the hallway past the busy nursing station. "Sure it is. But we'll have to sleep sometime."

"Separate rooms, Creighton," she warned, conceding that she'd already agreed to his harebrained scheme. "With a lock between them."

His subdued laughter as they stepped into the elevator was not in the least reassuring.

AT LAST, CURT HAD Kathryn Prim right where he wanted her—en route to a weekend in the most romantic city in the world, touted on page forty-three of the Seduction Incorporated catalog, as he recalled. Looking down at her curled-up figure asleep on the couch in his private jet, he considered all of the ways he'd like to make love to her. He recognized when he'd finally worked his way through a woman's defenses. Katie had been more resistant to his techniques than most—and would be worth the wait—but his efforts were about to pay off.

The problem, however, was that a damnable sense of nobility had begun to nag at Curt's conscience. How could he possibly take advantage of Kathryn when it had taken so long to gain at least a modicum of her trust?

Weary from the long hours at the hospital, he speared his fingers through his hair and grumbled a low, frustrated sound. *Separate rooms.*

Making his way to the cockpit, he thought about the call he had to make to his manager in Paris. He supposed the guy would be shocked when asked to discreetly arrange separate accommodations for Curt and his traveling companion. Well, he had been trying to deep-six the playboy image, hadn't he? This seemed like a damn good start—and incredibly lousy timing.

Somehow he'd have to protect Kathryn from the paparazzi, too. Those guys tended to watch incoming flights, and his private jet always attracted their attention.

A CHANCE LOST is one you may never have again.

Kathryn recalled Rudy's words all too clearly as the limousine belonging to Curt's corporate office in Paris edged its way through impossibly heavy afternoon traffic. Her dear friend and surrogate grandfather had lost his chance with the love of his life. Did Kathryn dare risk the same unending loneliness? Without any guarantees, she reminded herself.

She slid Curt a glance. He'd shaved, changed into a chambray shirt and slacks and looked wonderfully well rested. In contrast, she felt muddled by jet lag.

"Are we going directly to Antoinette's house?" she asked.

"That's the plan. We'll tell her about Rudy, give her a few hours to pack while we check into our hotel and we'll leave in the morning."

"I still think we should have called her from the States."

"She can't be a young woman and I didn't want to send her into shock. It's better if we tell her in person that Rudy's sick and then we can reassure her right away that he isn't in immediate danger."

It all sounded so logical the way Curt explained it, but somehow Kathryn felt the plan was flawed. Maybe between her concern for Rudy and loss of sleep she simply wasn't thinking too clearly.

One night in Paris. Not much time to spend in such a beautiful city, she mused, watching the passing scenery. All of the buildings looked so thoroughly European, as though they had been blown up to full-size from the pages of a travel brochure she might have studied during a moment of wishful thinking. In parks and along green belts, autumn had already kissed the leaves of hardwood trees with golden highlights. Pedestrians rushed along sidewalks, some of them businessmen hurrying to important appointments, she imagined, and others were clearly lovers out for an afternoon stroll. At every corner couples embraced, and at the myriad fountains scattered about the city she spotted more men and women caught up in romance. Acutely aware of Curt and his nearness, she envied the uninhibited show of affection the young couples displayed.

Paris . . . she sighed, the city of romance.

At home she never would have thought of kissing a man in public for fear someone she knew might see her. And talk. But here . . .

Not willing to pursue the thought to its ultimate conclusion, she craned her neck to get a better view out the car window. "Look! The Arc de Triomphe."

"Amazing" he drawled with a smile. "It's right where I left it last time I was here."

"Oh, you . . ." Laughing, she punched him lightly on the arm. "Don't tease. I'll gawk like a tourist if I want to. After all, I may never make it back to Paris." And might never have a chance to stroll arm in arm beside the Seine with the man she loved.

Loved? The word was there in her head as though it belonged, as though she'd known all along there was no other way she could feel about Curt. As though she was once more a foolish woman . . .

"We'll come whenever you want, Katie. Just name the day."

She intentionally covered her self-revelation with a flippant reply. "Life is too easy for you, Creighton. You ought to have to work for something so you can really appreciate it."

"Maybe you're right." He let his fingers stray to the back of her neck where he could toy with the loose strands of her hair. The sun slanting through the window shot each delicate thread with highlights of gold and red. Lovely. Perfection. He ached to release the band that held her hair back and feel the fine weight of silk in his hands. Better yet, he'd like to feel her hair spread across his bare chest, or see it cascading across a pillow where they slept. But he didn't dare hope for that.

"If we have time, I'll take you to the Eiffel Tower," he said. "Walking up to the top level will no doubt help us appreciate the view at sunset."

"That's not exactly what I meant by hard work."

"No? Then we must have coffee on the Champs Elysées. It's definitely hard work to watch all those beautiful Parisian women pass by." Though only Kathryn would hold his attention.

"You won't mind if I check out the men, will you?"

"Of course I will. We bachelor millionaires are a very insecure lot."

"Why is it I don't find that statement believable?"

Still looking out the window, she nestled against him and he caught her sweet floral scent. With an effort, he resisted nuzzling his lips along the slender column of her neck. Curt decided the hardest work of all was ignoring his instincts. He wanted Katie so badly it hurt. But it had to be her decision, not his.

Damn, but this being noble was a tough job!

Past the central city, the limousine turned off the main road into an elegant residential area with three-story, ivy-covered, shoulder-to-shoulder slate-gray homes, each one with lace curtains visible in the windows. The sharply sloped roofs boasted an array of chimneys. Few people were visible on the street, giving a visitor like Kathryn a sense that strangers weren't welcome. Admission came by invitation only to this wealthy enclave.

The driver slowed to a stop at mid-block and parked. "Number three-forty-two, *monsieur*," he announced, indicating the house on the right. "The Bilou residence."

"Thanks, Pierre. We shouldn't be long."

Curt got himself out of the car while the uniformed chauffeur assisted Kathryn. She smiled her thanks.

"How's your French?" she asked as Curt escorted her the few steps to the front door.

"Rusty, but we'll manage. I lived a year on the Left Bank studying photography. Although, come to think of it, my vocabulary was pretty well limited to telling half-naked models to smile and to ordering wine. That was in my wild, reckless youth, you understand."

Kathryn stifled a laugh. "A stage you haven't quite outgrown."

He shrugged and lifted the knocker.

A moment later a butler answered the door.

Curt's French was far too good for Kathryn to catch even the drift of the rather lengthy conversation. Only words like *Rudy* and *Marina Hospital* sounded familiar. Curt was full of surprises, she mused, and more modest about his language skills than she had expected. She was troubled, however, when the butler quietly closed the door, and she and Curt were still standing on the porch.

"What's wrong?"

"A slight miscalculation. Madame Bilou is visiting friends in the south of France."

"Ah, I suspected there was a flaw in this scheme of yours. What do we do now?" They'd come a heck of a long way to turn back now.

He glanced at his watch. "We check in at our hotel, get rid of our suitcases, then try for the Eiffel Tower at sunset. After that, a stroll through the Latin Quarter, I think, and finally dinner at an intimate little place I know."

She shook her head. "Shouldn't we be trying to reach Antoinette? Rudy's so sick..."

"Her butler is going to try to find her. I left him the number of our hotel." Curt slid his arm around her waist as they walked back to the limousine. "In the morning we'll fly down to Cannes to pick her up. We'll still be on schedule. You'll see."

When Curt made up his mind about something, he was simply irresistible. And how could Kathryn turn down an opportunity to see Paris? That really would be foolish. But no more so than the way she felt so thoroughly alive every time he touched her.

As she got into the car, she undid the clip that held her hair back. In this unfamiliar setting, with distinctively different architecture and a language she couldn't understand, a place where no one knew her, she felt amazingly relaxed. She shook her hair free.

For the first time in a dozen years, she decided to simply let life happen—no rigid, self-imposed constraints. This was, after all, Paris. Every woman deserved *one* night in the most romantic city in the world.

She cocked a look at Curt. Maybe what she was feeling had nothing to do with Paris. Maybe it had to do with Curt.

"I'd like to call the hospital to see how Rudy is," she said, not allowing herself to totally forget why they'd crossed the Atlantic.

"Sure. No problem. We'll call from the hotel."

"And then you can show me Paris." Anticipation curled through Kathryn, bringing her a new sense of buoyancy. Whatever the reason, she was glad to be in Paris with Curt and feeling the heated excitement of romance. Later, she vowed, she'd deal with any repercussions. Like guilt. Or the worry that somehow her father might learn what she'd been up to. Or the fact that she was about to blow the lid off the self-imposed restraints she'd lived with for most of her adult life.

"I hope you got enough sleep on the flight over, Curt, because we're going see everything and do everything until we both drop."

Chapter Eleven

"Come on, Curt. Don't be so slow." Laughing and all but dancing, Kathryn pulled Curt around to the other side of the Eiffel Tower viewing platform. "Look, you can see Notre Dame. It's like looking at the whole city in miniature from up here. Do you know the name of that church with the spires? Oh, isn't everything beautiful?"

Without waiting for his answer, or even a grunt of agreement, she pointed through the chain-link barrier to a slow-moving boat plowing its way through the darkening shadows on the Seine. "I wish we had time for a sight-seeing boat. But there's so much else to see and do." She was off again, like an impatient schoolgirl finally released for recess.

Curt had never seen her so animated. No staid Kathryn Prim now—she'd turned into an adventurous sprite, an energetic imp who couldn't stand still. Her infectious enthusiasm caught the other tourists off guard and they smiled at her indulgently.

The cooling breeze teased at her hair, sending flyaway strands of gold and red across her face. She brushed them out of the way. In the setting rays of sunlight, the subdued rose shade of her simple dress took on a vibrant hue. Mirth sparkled in her eyes, and when she smiled up at Curt, he felt a tightening of muscles low in his body and a strange constriction inside his chest. God, she was beautiful, ripe with the fullness of womanhood.

So very different and far more special than any woman he had ever known before.

She looked out across the skyline again, sighed deeply, then announced, "Let's catch the next elevator down. I want to go to the Champs Elysées now. You promised me a cup of coffee."

"That's it for the Eiffel Tower?" he asked incredulously, reluctant to give up the incredible sight of Kathryn with the whole of Paris as her backdrop. Pity he hadn't thought to bring along his camera. He wanted to capture her spirit on film, though it would take a true artist to do her justice.

"You mean I paid the exorbitant admission price to this amazing tourist attraction," he grumbled good-naturedly, "and you've seen everything you wanted to see in ten minutes?"

"Time's the most valuable commodity right now." She stood on tiptoe to plant a flirtatious kiss on his cheek. "And I plan to spend each minute wisely, Mr. Creighton, bachelor millionaire extraordinaire. I certainly hope you can keep up."

"I'll manage." An admiring grin tugged at the corners of his lips. He wasn't entirely sure he could handle this "new" Katie.

Once back on ground level, she hurried him into a taxi, announcing their destination to the driver in absolutely rotten French. For once the cabbie didn't seem to mind his mother country's language being botched. Who could resist someone as irresistible as Katie Prim?

The driver let them off in front of a fashion design house on the boulevard, and Curt commented, "Sorry the stores are closed. I'd buy you an elegant gown for a keepsake if I could."

"Don't be silly." She slid her arm around his waist, and with his arm he circled her shoulder. "What would I do back home with a designer dress? Wear it to lectures on corporate law? I'd much rather stroll along the sidewalk, enjoying the ambience. You can almost taste the romance in the air, can't you? Isn't it wonderful?"

Curt could smell her light fragrance and figured that beat the hell out of the vehicle exhaust from passing cars. Katie didn't seem to notice. And the fact that she truly didn't seem in the least disappointed that she wouldn't own a Paris original shouldn't have surprised him. But he'd known a lot of women. For most, however they might protest otherwise, the trappings of wealth were important fringe benefits only a man like Curt could provide. Katie was different. She simply didn't give a damn.

Amazing.

As they walked, her hip hugged hard against Curt's and her leg brushed his slacks-clad thigh with each step. The rhythmic contact created a vibration from skin to bone to visceral awareness that set Curt's teeth on edge—among other parts of his anatomy. He wondered if she knew what she was doing to him. And decided it didn't matter. If she kept up this assault on his senses, no amount of resolve would keep his baser instincts in check.

As they attempted to cross an intersection, Katie paid particular attention to the sculptured water fountain at the center of the traffic circle, leading Curt around the greenstone cherubs twice before halting. The intricately formed statue glistened with water in the lights from the passing cars.

"Have you noticed all the fountains in Paris?" she asked with a wistful note in her voice. "How many do you suppose there are?"

"I don't know that anyone has bothered to count them."

"I wish we could."

"Why would you want to do that?"

"Because I've been watching, and young couples always stop beside a fountain to kiss. It's like a ritual. If you and I could count the fountains together, then we'd be able to kiss a hundred times. Maybe even a thousand times."

The tightness in Curt's chest grew to giant proportions and filled his throat with emotion. Her eyes held such longing, so much need, he ached to ease her pain. And his own. "If that's the case, I'm ready to start counting right now."

With a wickedly sexy smile, she slid her arms up his chest and linked them behind his neck. "It's so sad we only have one night in Paris."

"We'll find a way to make the most of it." That was a promise, Curt told himself as he lowered his head in response to her open invitation. Whatever she wanted, however much she wanted, he was more than willing to grant her wish. Her soft, sweet lips parted in eager welcome and he plunged his tongue into the warm depths. Exciting, exhilarating, she tasted of the bright lights of a Paris evening, the vibrant colors of autumn, the flavor of romance.

She pressed herself against him, her breasts soft mounds that singed through layers of clothing to burn him. She nudged into the cradle of his hips and he groaned a low, throaty sound. Need rocketed through him.

"Sweet Katie, if you keep this up I'm going to embarrass us both."

"It doesn't look to me like Parisians embarrass easily."

"Well, I do." He'd never imagined Katie kissing with such uninhibited verve while standing in the middle of a public sidewalk. *Private* Kathryn Prim would never have acted so spontaneously, in fact, she had electrified him in a way he had never previously envisioned. Sweat suddenly beaded his forehead.

Taking her by the shoulders, he fought for control. "Let's get that cup of coffee," he pleaded.

"And see if we can find a few more fountains to count?" she asked mischievously. Womanly self-confidence sparkled in her eyes. She was set on seducing him, Curt realized, one torturous step at a time.

The hell with nobility! Because of Kathryn he'd been carrying around a supply of condoms for weeks. He hoped to God he'd get to use them. Soon.

One cup of coffee and three fountains later, Curt decided it was likely to be a very long, painful evening. She had him in a constant state of arousal. It wasn't just her kisses that were driving him crazy. At every opportunity she touched him. At the café her hand had been busy under the table nonchalantly stroking his thigh, and causing him to grind his teeth in order to contain the urge to toss her over his shoulder and haul her back to the hotel. As they walked along, he never knew when she was going to brush her fingertips to his face in a caress that was half sexy and half innocent. Or curl her fingers through his hair. And every time she did, he had to fight the explosive need that gripped him.

She had him totally off balance and unprepared for whatever new stunt she had up her sleeve.

Even a short taxi ride turned into a full-scale erotic adventure that left him gasping for air when she hopped out to gaze at the next tourist attraction.

Damn! Where had she learned to be so innately provocative? And how had she managed to keep all that sensuality bottled up for twelve years? He'd suspected since the first night he met Katie that she was a passionate woman. Now she was peeling away her staid, professional image layer by enticing layer, like a skilled stripper teases her audience into a frenzy. In this case it was an audience of one—namely him. And he was very nearly coming unglued.

The woman Katie was revealing was even more intriguing than the one he had pursued these past few weeks.

Along Montmartre Place du Tertre, a young artist with a narrow face and well-rehearsed patter lured Katie to his easel set up in the light from a café. "A portrait, *mademoiselle,*" he offered. "For your memories of Paris. Only a few francs."

She gave Curt a questioning look and he shrugged. "If you'd like," he said. He doubted he'd ever be able to deny her the slightest wish. Certainly not tonight.

"Do make me beautiful," she urged the artist, laughing and taking a seat in the chair opposite the young man.

"With your beauty, *mademoiselle,* my task is *très* simple."

Curt felt a sudden stab of jealousy. He didn't want any other man to make her smile so radiantly. Only he should be allowed that privilege.

As she unconsciously licked her lips, Curt had to wonder at the power of that simple gesture and the instant reaction of his body.

In a few quick strokes of colored chalk, Kathryn saw her portrait emerging on the sketch pad, the laughing, smiling image of a woman in love. Was she so transparent? she wondered. Or was the artist that perceptive? He'd caught the glow in her cheeks she'd been feeling all evening, the glitter of joy reflected in her eyes. Perhaps in Paris, artists were trained to depict women through romance-tinted glasses.

She glanced up at Curt. Could he possibly know what she was feeling, too?

He was the cause of her joy, she realized. It was because of him she felt suddenly freed of the constraints she had worn like a sackcloth all these years. If she'd been alone in Paris, the newness of it all would have made her nervous; with any other companion her carefully nurtured reserve and caution would have remained very much intact. But not with Curt. With him she felt liberated.

With a dramatic flourish, the artist signed and dated his work. "Now you shall not forget your visit to Paris," he promised.

The bittersweet realization that one night in Paris—one night with Curt—would never be enough, constricted her throat. "No, I won't forget."

THEY ARRIVED BACK at the hotel very late—Kathryn only slightly tipsy from the wine she'd consumed with dinner.

She giggled when Curt fumbled with the key, trying to open the door to her room. "I'm the one who's drunk, not you."

The key slid into the slot and he opened the door with a courtly bow. "Absolutely, *mademoiselle*. A true Frenchman never gets drunk."

"I didn't know you were French."

"My adopted country. Same thing."

"Of course."

He pressed on her the souvenirs they'd collected during the evening. "Your portrait. I assure you, it does not do you justice."

She accepted the rolled sketch, knowing she would treasure the memories it represented.

"And this." From his pocket he withdrew a champagne glass.

She giggled again. "Such a naughty boy. But then I suppose I shouldn't have made you take that from the restaurant."

"Not to worry. I'll send them a generous check in the morning." He ran the back of his fingers lightly down her cheek, his blue-green eyes gazing at her with undisguised hunger that equaled her own. "I only regret we ran out of fountains to admire."

Acutely aware of the large, inviting bed in the room behind her, Kathryn staunchly ignored a sudden flutter of anxiety. She had atoned for her sins for twelve long years, perversely avoiding even the slightest hint of scandal and denying her own basic needs. Surely she'd earned one night of love.

"We could pretend," she suggested, her voice rough and filled with emotion.

"That there's a fountain in the hallway?"

Stepping inside, she held the door open wide. "I think we'd do better in here."

"Katie . . ." He cleared his throat. "If I come in there, I won't be able to stop at a kiss."

She didn't hesitate. "I want you, Curt." Her voice was low and sultry, a husky invitation. "I have for a very long time."

In one long stride, Curt was in the room, shoving the door shut behind him with a kick of his foot. His hands shook as he framed her face. "Katie, my sweet, sweet Katie." He groaned.

"Please, Curt. It's been so long."

His mouth found hers with a new urgency. He'd waited, too. Forever, it seemed, for this chance to explore the full range of Katie's sensuality. But he had to go slow, he warned himself. In spite of her eagerness, twelve years of abstinence made this almost like the first time for her. He wanted to make it good, no quick adolescent act that was over as fast as it had begun. He'd always prided himself on his self-control. Katie, her busy fingers already unbuttoning his shirt, would put him to the test.

Slowly, he thought with grim determination as she slid his shirt off his shoulders. If she would cooperate.

Kathryn needed to touch him—the warmth of his skin, the springy cinnamon brown hair on his chest, his nipples that puckered as she skimmed her palms over his magnificent body. Passion long denied ached for release within her. She wanted this man—this sexy, persistent, undeniably virile male—to hold her and fill her and make her feel like a woman as only he could. Her desire was so great she was dizzy with it, dizzy with the sensation of him effortlessly lifting her dress over her head, of his long, tapered fingers slipping straps from her shoulders, of being bare to his hungry perusal.

She groaned when his lips touched and teased, then gently suckled at her breast. "Curt..." She speared her fingers through his hair and drew him closer.

His teeth raked tenderly across her sensitive flesh. "Curt, I can't..."

"I know, sweetheart. I know." With easy insistence, he helped her shed the remainder of her clothes. In sibilant whispers, each bit of fabric dropped to puddle on the lushly carpeted floor.

"Beautiful." Like an artist, he drew his fingertips over the lines of her breasts, her waist and the intimate curve of her hip. "Truly lovely."

She couldn't catch her breath or find her voice. In the light cast by a single bed lamp, her senses seemed magnified. They collided one with another in hedonistic pleasure—the salty taste of his skin, his purely masculine scent, the hum of low, throaty sounds that might have been made by him . . . or her.

With shaking hands, she shoved at the waistband of his slacks. "It's not fair if I can't see you, too."

With a swift intake of air, he lifted her in his arms and delivered her to the oversize bed, its satin quilt pulled back to reveal pristine white sheets. "I'll take care of that little detail in due time."

"But I want to touch you. There."

"Later, Katie. Later you can touch me anywhere you want. But not just yet. I'm afraid I'd burst if you did."

She felt a smug, thoroughly feminine smile curl her lips. She had forgotten—or perhaps she'd never fully understood—how satisfying it was to have a man want her so much that he was afraid he'd lose control.

A moment later, when Curt's hand slid into the triangle of curls at the apex of her thighs, Kathryn's arrogant boast shattered like a fine crystal glass. She was the one out of control. She'd never felt such heat, so much trembling need. "Now, Curt. I want you now."

"Not yet. Not till I've driven you crazy, sweetheart. Just like you've been driving me wild all night long."

"Cruel . . ." she sobbed between shuddering breaths. "Really cruel."

"Yeah. And you're going to love every minute."

His warm, teasing laughter played on her senses as erotically as his talented fingers stroked her body to new heights of self-awareness. He found erogenous zones she hadn't known existed and taught her how amazingly responsive she could be to a man skilled in the art of love.

She didn't know when he shed his clothes, or if she'd had a part in it. She knew only the way the masculine texture of his skin felt beneath her hands, the taste of him in her mouth and his distinctive scent that was fast becoming a part of her.

"Curt!" Only after she cried out his name in explosive release did he give her the final satisfaction of joining their bodies together in a perfect fit. Hard against soft. Conquest and submission in equal amounts.

"Katie!" With a groan, he mimicked her plea and she felt him shudder in her arms. The satisfied sounds she made at the back of her throat mixed with the call of her name in consummate harmony.

For a while their heavy breathing rasped loudly in the room, a duet of satisfaction that slowly quieted into a contented sigh.

Finally Curt propped himself up on his elbows. The half-amazed, well-satisfied look in Katie's hazel eyes brought a sudden wave of tenderness to his heart. For the first time in his life he held a woman in his arms he never wanted to let go. Not ever. And he wasn't in the least confident she felt the same way.

"I must be crushing you," he said.

"I don't mind. You feel good." She finger combed his hair back from his forehead. "Usually... before... I didn't know it could be like this."

He rolled to his back, bringing her with him so she was on top. "If it's any consolation, I didn't know, either, sweetheart."

"You didn't miss that big round bed of yours in the guest room?"

"Not a chance."

"Or the mirror?"

"Katie, I told you I never used that room. I swear—"

"I know." With a troubled sigh, she slid to his side and rested her head on his shoulder, her hand on his chest where she could feel the steady beat of his heart.

"What's wrong?" he asked softly.

She wondered if she had the courage to tell him all the details of her sordid past. And what he'd think of her if she did.

"Don't freeze up on me, honey. There's nothing in the world you can tell me that's going to change how I feel about you."

"Are you a mind reader?"

"No, but I could sure feel you withdrawing from me. I'm not going to let that happen. No turning into an ice maiden, Katie. Not this time." He brushed a kiss to her hair. "It's still those guys in high school who gave you such a hard time, isn't it?"

"Partly," she admitted. "When I got..." She swallowed hard. "I was pregnant when I left Waverly."

The silence hung painfully in the air with Kathryn holding her breath for what felt like an eternity. Waiting for Curt's reaction was like waiting for a time bomb to go off. She never should have admitted—

"Ah, honey," he soothed, "that must have scared you to death." He squeezed her so hard, with such deep caring, she almost cried in relief. "What about the guy? He just let you go off on your own?"

"He denied everything."

"You could have proved his paternity. Blood tests and all."

"By that time, I didn't even want him to be the father of my child. I'd been such a fool." She drew a shaky breath. Obviously, as an adolescent, she'd confused sex with love. She hoped she hadn't repeated the same error some twelve years later. "I left Waverly because my father threw me out of the house."

Curt sat bolt upright. "Your father threw you out? His own kid? When you were in trouble?"

He looked so offended, Kathryn almost laughed, but the depth of her father's betrayal still hurt too much. "He's the local bank president, elder in the biggest church in town and, generally, the self-appointed keeper of morality in all of Waverly. Image was everything for my father. It wasn't simply that I had gotten pregnant. Word of my fallen-woman status had spread all over town. He couldn't handle that."

Curt let loose a string of expletives that would have stunned the members of her father's church. "I'll kill him. So help me, I'll kill him."

Kathryn touched two fingers to his lips. "Don't. It wouldn't help."

"My God, Katie, how did you survive?"

"He gave me half an hour to get out of the house. I used the time to pack and filch the extra cash I knew he kept hidden in his desk. Then I hopped a bus to L.A." She shuddered at the memory and her stomach churned. "About three years later, I sent him a money order for the amount I'd taken. I didn't include a return address."

"That phone call you were making the night we met? To your sister?"

"I've been trying to build up the courage to face that part of my life again...and to see my father."

In almost a growl, Curt said, "I'm not sure he's worth it."

"He's the only father I've got," she persisted. "And I do miss my sister."

Curt pulled her into his arms and simply held her, held her in the way she'd wanted to be held twelve years ago. Then she'd had no one. Now she had Curt.

"The baby, sweetheart," he said after a while, so quietly she almost didn't hear his voice. "What happened to the baby? How did you manage?"

"I was lucky. I made my way to a home for unwed mothers, and after the baby came I relinquished her for adoption. I didn't have my high-school diploma. No job. No prospects. I wanted more for her than I had to give. There hasn't been a day since when I didn't think of her. And not many when I didn't have to force myself not to cry."

"Do you have any contact with her?"

She shook her head. "When she's grown up... If she wants to, she'll be able to find me. I wouldn't want to disrupt her life now, or her family, or hurt her in any way."

"I understand how you feel, honey. About the baby and all. As much as any man can, I understand."

Kathryn believed him and that lifted a burden she'd carried a long time. She snuggled against his hard, masculine body, letting him absorb some of the pain she'd shouldered alone for so many years. Tension that had kept her an emotional prisoner drained away as she drifted off to sleep in his arms.

She didn't know how long she lay like that, warm and secure in his embrace. More than once, Curt woke her with gentle caresses that quickly unleashed a full range of passionate responses. A skilled lover, he thought of her needs first, never leaving her wanting—until an hour or so later, when he would adroitly resurrect desires she thought he had fully satisfied.

Eventually her eyes fluttered open on their own. Though she knew it was daylight, the heavy drapes on the hotel windows allowed only a trace of sunlight into the room. She couldn't guess the time.

Gingerly, she shifted her position and discovered she was the tiniest bit tender in the most intimate of places. Kathryn's smile was profoundly feminine as memories of her night with Curt came flooding back. He was undoubtedly the most sensual man she had ever met—or ever hoped to meet. Everything he did—his kisses, his touch, his voice, his dimpled grin, the wicked sparkle in his eyes—was created for a woman to feast upon. She imagined she would never tire of the banquet of hedonistic pleasures he provided.

"Mornin', Katie."

"Hmm." She cuddled closer, loving the raspy way he said her name in his sleepy morning voice. "I suppose it's time to go get Antoinette."

"I was thinking there'd be time for us to take a shower first." His palm slid down along her back and he cupped her buttocks.

Deep inside, her body clenched in reaction to his familiar touch. Perhaps her one glorious night in Paris wasn't quite over yet. "May I assume you mean for us to take that shower together?"

"You assume correctly, Ms. Prim. I always knew you were a clever girl."

She let her hand drift across his flat belly, finally letting it wander to the evidence of his arousal. "And you, Mr. Creighton, have an astounding amount of endurance."

He made a little choking sound as she gently closed her fingers around him. "Must be all those aerobics classes I've been attending lately."

"Very possibly. Or all that tennis. Speaking of which, I still can't figure out how you and the twins managed to beat Stefan."

"Well...I have kind of a confession to make about that."

She lifted her head from his chest. "Confession?"

"I sort of bribed him to throw the match."

"You didn't!"

"I was a desperate man. I didn't want to lose our wager, so I fixed him up on a date with the twins in exchange for a few missed shots."

"Oh, you men! You don't know how to play fair." Not really angry, she dug her fingertips into his ribs. "Lucy said you were ticklish. Let's see if she was right."

"Hey, no. Don't do that." Laughing, he tried to escape her roving fingers.

"You deserve worse than this for cheating." She added an old-fashioned stomach blow to his punishment. "How about that day I went to your house? Did you bribe Clarence Middlebury, the other paralegal, to stay home sick?"

"No, no. That was pure good luck."

"There's nothing pure about you, Creighton." She tortured him further.

"Stop! I call a truce!"

In one swift, athletic movement, he was on his feet with Kathryn in his arms, en route to the bathroom. Walls of mirrors reflected marble counters and gleaming brass fixtures that bounced back the sound of laughter filling the room.

Moments later, warm water, billowing suds and Curt's familiar hands slicked over Kathryn in a cascade of carnal delight until she was drowning in the sensations he created.

"Enough," she pleaded breathlessly. Her legs lacked the strength to hold her upright.

"It'll never be enough." Lifting Kathryn so she could wrap her legs around his waist, Curt slid into her with a powerful stroke that brought cries of pleasure from them both.

Chapter Twelve

Possessive. Protective. That's how he felt. Responsible, too. And filled with pride that Katie had shared with him both her passion and her secrets.

Walking with easy strides across the hotel lobby, Curt figured this was as good as it got. A terrific woman beside him. A night to remember. And—

Damn!

He spotted the guy lurking behind one of those man-eating indoor plants. A photographer. A freelance joker from the States known for selling his wares to the highest bidder and sleaziest tabloids— Bernie Zimmer.

Doing a quick one-eighty, Curt ushered Kathryn down a corridor in the opposite direction.

"Where are we going?" she asked. "I thought we were going to check out."

"We are. I just have to, ah, check on something first."

She seemed to accept his explanation, until he led them through an empty banquet room and into the hotel's stainless-steel kitchen that was bustling with activity.

"Curt, are you planning to play some kind of a trick on me? Like make me wash the dishes to pay off our bill?"

"Not a chance, sweetheart." He found a spot for her out of the way of all the hustle and bustle, and placed their small pieces of carry-on luggage next to her. "Stay right here. Don't budge an inch and I'll be right back."

A scowl pleated her forehead. "What's going on? Why can't I go with you?"

He brushed a kiss against her lips. "Trust me."

Hurrying away before she could make further objection, Curt soon found a young Frenchman who looked like the sort he needed—someone ambitious who knew the value of money. Their conversation was short and to the point. Once in agreement, Curt peeled off a good many bills from the stash of U.S. dollars he had in his pocket. In exchange, he received a set of car keys.

"A Fiat?" Kathryn questioned a few minutes later as Curt helped her into the vintage car. "What happened to the limousine?"

"Pierre was busy."

"I thought he was your employee. Couldn't you simply tell him to pick us up?"

"I don't like to take advantage." He tossed their gear in the back seat and squeezed in behind the wheel.

"But where did this car come from? It's not exactly what I expected a company car from Creighton Enterprises to look like."

"I borrowed it from a friend." When the darn thing took three tries to start, and then missed on a couple of cylinders, Curt decided his *friend* had conned him.

"This is very strange, Curt. You decide not to check out of the hotel—"

"They'll bill the company credit card."

"Then you borrow an old clunker that sounds like it's ready for the junkyard."

"It'll warm up in a minute."

"Why do I have the distinct feeling you're not telling me something? Like I'm being kidnapped?"

He gave her an oblique look and grinned. "Damn! Why didn't I think of that?"

"Curt..." she warned.

"All right. All right." He maneuvered the car out of the cramped parking slot into the heavy, slow-moving traffic. "There was a photographer waiting for us in the lobby."

"A photog—" She made a pathetic mewling sound at the back of her throat and sank deeper into the bucket seat. "I don't want my picture in the papers, Curt. I really don't."

"Precisely why we made a hasty departure, sweetheart. To dodge the guy."

"Thank you." The color had drained from her cheeks. Her hands trembled and she folded them primly in her lap. "I can just imagine what my father would say if it was splashed all over the tabloids that I spent the weekend in Paris with you."

"Yeah. Sure." Gritting his teeth, Curt turned right at the end of the block. "Has it occurred to you that you're twenty-nine years old and what your father thinks, or doesn't think, shouldn't matter anymore?"

"It's not just my father. It's..." She verbally stumbled in search of another excuse. "The people I work with."

"Your co-workers can damn well mind their own business." He slammed on the brakes to avoid colliding with a taxi. "Maybe you're just plain ashamed to be seen hanging around with me."

She placed her hand on his thigh. "That's not it, Curt. You know it's not. Please try to understand."

"I'm trying." He really was. But it hurt like hell that he wanted to shout from the rooftops that he and Katie Prim were meant for each other, while she wanted to keep their relationship a dark little secret.

He glanced into the rearview mirror and swore under his breath. Bernie was back.

"What's wrong?"

"The guy I was telling you about must have spotted us leaving the hotel. He's in that cab about two cars behind us."

She whipped her head around. "Curt..."

"Stay out of sight. I'll lose him." Curt edged the Fiat between the curb and stalled traffic, then took a hard right into an alley. As he accelerated down the narrow service road, a restaurant worker dumping garbage in a trash bin had to duck out of the way or get clipped by a fender. The taxi that followed got the brunt of the Frenchman's colorful language.

At the end of the alley, Curt was met with a wall of unmoving traffic. He took a left onto the sidewalk. Pedestrians sprinted for safety in a dozen different directions.

"Curt! You're going to kill someone."

"Everything's under control."

He bounded off the curb and across an intersection, then did a quick U-turn when oncoming cars filled all the lanes. With a gasp, Kathryn put her arm in front of her face as though to ward off the inevitable crash. Curt hadn't counted on so many one-way streets, all of them jammed with traffic and none of them going where he wanted to go—which was away from the pursuing paparazzi.

But Curt had played this game before.

Remembering his student days, he crossed the Seine and wove his way through the narrow streets of the Left Bank. He checked his mirror regularly and glanced in both directions at every intersection.

"I think we lost 'em," he said, finally slowing to a pace that matched the rest of the traffic. "You okay?"

"Sure, if you're not concerned about my heart palpitations and the fact that my entire life has flashed in front of my eyes about six times in the past ten minutes."

He leaned his head back and laughed in a burst of released tension. "You're the greatest, Katie Prim. Terrific."

"Thanks. I think. Personally, I'm relieved to still be in one piece." She wiped her palms on her slacks. "But now what? Are we still going to fly to Cannes to pick up Antoinette?"

Shaking his head, Curt said, "I don't think that's a good idea. That photographer was probably alerted when we landed, and he'll have someone watching the airport. When we get out of this mess of traffic, I'll find a place to make a few phone calls. I figure we can drive south and have Jackson and the plane meet us at Cannes."

"That'll take hours for us to drive that far, won't it?"

"We'll still have time to get you back to L.A. before you have to be at work. You can catch up on your sleep in the plane." Though Curt could think of a lot better ways they could spend their time.

SOME MINUTES LATER, after he'd located a public phone, Curt realized he had seriously misjudged the efficiency of his flight crew, the loyalty of French butlers and the determination of Antoinette Bilou.

"What do you mean we're stranded in France?" Kathryn asked when he returned to the car where she'd been waiting, pacing up and down on the sidewalk.

"It's only temporary. It seems Antoinette's butler tried to call me last night. Since I wasn't in my room..." He let the words trail off, enjoying the quick blush that swept up Kathryn's cheeks as she remembered where they'd been and what they'd been doing when he missed the call. "Anyway, he took matters into his own hands. He reached Jackson, my pilot, and got him to fly to Cannes to pick up *madame*. Jackson flew her directly back to the States."

"A very conscientious employee."

"Absolutely. He knew why we'd come to France." And knew Curt was hoping for an excuse to stay an extra day or more with Kathryn—but Curt wasn't about to admit that to her. He did plan to give Jackson a bonus, however, for his quick thinking. "Based on his conversation with the butler, he figured we were planning to go to Cannes. He left word he'd meet us there tomorrow."

"Tomorrow?"

"With a fresh crew, of course."

"But, Curt, I have to be at work tomorrow."

He shrugged. "You can call in sick. Better yet, you can tell Tom the truth—that the two of us are having a terrific time in France."

She looked aghast. "I can't do that! He's my boss. And he's very, very conservative."

"My guess is that Lucy is trying to rectify that little shortcoming of his. And having some success, too."

Kathryn didn't buy into his idea. "We can take a commercial flight home."

Folding his arms across his chest and leaning his hips back against the Fiat, he said, "Sure, if that's what you want. Of course, that photographer and his buddies are likely to be hanging around the airport. Doesn't bother me. It wouldn't be the first time my mug shot hit the front page of some tabloid."

"You enjoy putting me in impossible situations, don't you, Creighton?"

He grinned. "Ease up, sweetheart. It's a beautiful day, and we have a chance to see some of the loveliest countryside in the world. Why not relax and enjoy it?''

Kathryn fumed and fussed, but what could she do? She was stuck. And if truth be known, somewhere deep in her heart she wanted to rejoice. She'd made an honest effort to get back to work on time. She'd come to France to help out her friend, Rudy. Things hadn't quite worked out as she had expected, or planned, but her intentions had certainly been virtuous. Perhaps she was simply being rewarded for her good deed with one more day in France.

Drawing a deep breath of brisk air touched with the promise of winter, she rubbed her arms and said, ''How many hours to Cannes?''

The victorious smile that creased both of his cheeks did fluttery things to Kathryn's midsection. ''As many as you would like, sweet Katie.''

She hoped she wouldn't have to pay too high a price for her indiscretions.

VINEYARDS PAINTED with autumn reds and golds stretched to the horizon through a rainy mist. The Fiat's windshield wipers smeared half-moon paths across the dirty glass. The heater didn't work at all.

''I think we should have listened to the weather report this morning,'' Kathryn mused aloud as she peered at the murky view. The lovely day had deteriorated into a gloomy, overcast afternoon.

"We had other, much more important things to do."

"Locating a road map would have been a clever use of our time." The narrow, unpaved road Curt had turned onto sometime back was clearly not a shortcut to the high-speed route to Cannes.

"Surely you're not suggesting we should have skipped our shower in favor of finding a map."

"Not exactly." She squirmed in the seat, trying to find a more comfortable position. The rough road was compounding a serious problem with the car's shock absorbers. "I just thought it would have saved us time in the long run if we knew where we were going."

"Where's your sense of adventure?"

"I think I left it back on the streets of Paris where you almost killed those pedestrians, not to mention us."

"Stick with me, sweet Katie." He laughed. "I've got a real treat in store for you."

The car chose that moment to cough twice, lurch forward with a final wheeze, then silently roll to a stop on the deserted road. Grimly, Curt twisted the ignition key, which caused the wipers to get out of sync. They locked together like dueling swordsmen in the middle of the windshield.

Kathryn's lips twitched at the corners. Curt looked so glum, she didn't dare laugh out loud. "A real treat?"

"We're out of gas."

"Really?" she teased. "I never would have guessed."

He gave her a sullen look. "The gauge must be broken."

"Everything else on the car seems to be. I can't think why the gauge would work when nothing else does."

He slammed the heel of his hand into the steering wheel. "If I ever catch that kid who sold me this piece of junk, I swear I'll string him up by his ears!"

"You *bought* it? I thought..." She choked back another laugh.

"Yeah, well, at the time it seemed like the smart thing to do." He glanced out the window. "Let's try over there. Maybe we can get some help." He pointed to the shadowy shape of a building a few hundred feet away. It didn't look like a place of refuge to Kathryn.

She shrugged. "Whatever you say, Curt, but my guess is we're going to have to walk back to the main road."

Once out of the car, he took her hand and they ran through a mist as soft as dew on a chilly morning. He lifted her over a low rock fence, his hands at her waist, his thumbs just brushing the curves of her breasts. Her breath caught in her throat. Before their night in Paris, Kathryn hadn't truly known what pleasure a man's touch could bring her. Now her body seemed ultrasensitive to the least bit of contact.

The building he led her to was low to the ground, built of rocks and didn't have a single window. The door was padlocked shut.

"Not much help for us here," Kathryn pointed out.

"We'll see." He fussed with the lock until it popped open.

She cocked her head. "How'd you do that?"

"Picking locks is an old hobby of mine. I used to break into Lucy's diary all the time when we were kids."

Kathryn sputtered.

As he shoved open the heavy door, she said, "I'm really not into breaking and entering, Curt. Why don't we just walk back to the road?"

"We'd get all wet."

"We'd also avoid being locked away in some dank and dreary French prison for the rest of our lives."

"Maybe I could bribe them to assign us to the same dungeon." He gave her a quick wink.

Suppressing a smile, she gave a "humph" of disapproval. The thought of being locked up with Curt

for the rest of her life did have a certain appeal—
though she wasn't about to admit it to him.

Miraculously he found a switch that turned on the
lights. A dozen stairs led down to a huge room filled
with rows of barrels stacked three high. The tangy
scent of fermenting fruit filled the air.

"A wine cellar," she announced.

"Looks like." Nonchalantly he wandered down
the row, examining the oak casks. The light from the
bare bulbs glistened off his damp hair, haloing it in
red. Kathryn had to fight the sensation that tightened her chest. He was such a beautiful man, so full
of life and vitality it took her breath away.

"This one looks like a good year," he said, rapping his knuckles on the barrel. "It's full, too."

"Curt, I don't think we ought to be messing
around with their wine."

Ignoring her, Curt tapped into the cask he'd selected. "See if you can find us a couple of glasses,
sweetheart."

"I'll do no such thing! I think we ought to get out
of here before someone catches us. Frenchmen are
bound to be fussy about who helps themselves to
samples of their wine."

Undaunted, he wandered off down the row of
casks, returning a few minutes later with two glasses.
He filled the glass with an inch of deep, rose-colored

liquid, swirled it and held it up to the light. He sniffed, then sipped the wine.

"Ninety-one was definitely a good year for cabernet sauvignon. Nice, rich color. Superior bouquet. Very smooth." He filled the second glass, pressed it into her hand and lifted his in a toast. "To us, Ms. Prim. And to our tour of France." A beguiling smile deepened the creases in his cheeks.

"I suppose we can't pour it back in the cask?"

"Probably not."

"To us," she echoed with little conviction. Though she might love Curt, they were an unlikely pair. He relished the spotlight; she preferred the anonymity of the shadows. Given both his wealth and his charismatic personality, she could see little chance of finding middle ground. And she'd never try to force him into a mold that would quash his effervescence, for that's what she loved the most. He made her smile.

She sipped the wine, letting it slide smoothly down her throat past the painful constriction she felt. Unshed tears burned at the backs of her eyes. "It's lovely," she agreed.

He gazed at her over the top of his glass. "So are you."

Taking a second sip, she concentrated on the taste of the wine, trying to force away a sudden wash of hopeless melancholy. "Exquisite."

"Yes, you are."

At the husky tone of his voice, she raised her gaze to meet his. While she'd been contemplating the impossible, he'd stepped closer—so close, she could see the fan of his unfairly long lashes and the tiny gold specks in his blue-green eyes. His expressive eyebrows naturally formed an arrogant arch and his nose appeared aristocratic; but it was the way his smile gentled the strong shape of his jaw that made her heartbeat accelerate.

"Have you ever made love in a wine cellar?" he asked. Dipping his head, he brushed a kiss at that sensitive spot right below her ear, an erogenous zone he'd explored at length last night, and again this morning.

A shiver raced down her spine. "Not that I can recall."

"Conjures up some interesting possibilities, doesn't it?" He nibbled on her earlobe.

She canted her head to give him better access to all the tender places along her neck she wanted him to investigate. "The floor looks a little uncomfortable. Too hard, I imagine."

His tongue swirled around the shell of her ear. "Maybe we could stretch out on top of the casks."

"Too lumpy." Her eyes fluttered shut and a pleasant lethargy invaded her limbs. Curt had the most talented tongue, she mused, and he used it in masterful ways.

"There's a tasting table in the back. You'd be a perfect vintage." He placed a dozen feather-light kisses on her eyelids. "A little on the sweet side, perhaps, but with an appealing bite."

She wavered, her legs no longer steady beneath her. She leaned back until she felt the rim of a wooden barrel press against her shoulders and thighs. She envisioned herself lying naked on an ancient oak table, Curt tasting her in all sorts of intimate ways.

His breath warmed her face; his words heated her imagination.

"On the other hand," he whispered against her lips, "a feather bed would be nice."

"Feather bed?" she asked with a sigh. "In a wine cellar?"

His tongue teased at the corners of her lips. "At the château."

"What château?"

"The one that's a quarter of a mile up the road. A hundred rooms, thirty of them bedrooms. Frescoes on the ceilings. Some of them downright suggestive." He nipped seductively at her bottom lip between each pronouncement. "You'll love it."

"Hmm. Sounds heavenly." What was truly heavenly was how Curt made her feel. Extraordinarily feminine. Achingly desirable.

And thoroughly puzzled.

Frowning, she shoved at his unyielding chest. "How do you know so much about this particular château?" she asked suspiciously.

"I own it."

"You what?"

"More accurately, it's Creighton Enterprises that owns the vineyard and the château. This is where we get some of the private label wines we advertise in the Seduction Incorporated catalog."

"No!"

His grin contained not the least amount of remorse. "'Fraid so. I'd say this vintage—" he held up the wine they had sipped together "—is going to be imminently successful."

"You conned me again, Creighton," she wailed. "You weren't lost on that dinky little road trying to find some stupid shortcut. You knew where you were going all the time."

"Naturally."

"You had me scared to death that we were going to get shot for trespassing."

"You should have trusted me."

"Like a chicken trusts a fox." She planted her fists on her hips. "I'm going to get you for this, Creighton."

"I certainly hope so."

She rolled her eyes. The man was absolutely impossible. And totally irresistible.

Behind Kathryn, someone discreetly cleared his throat.

"*Bonjour,* Monsieur Creighton. *Mademoiselle.*" Hat in hand, the burly workman bowed with great dignity. "Welcome to the vineyards of Château Amour. I trust I am not disturbing your wine tasting."

"Not at all, Jacques. You're right on time." Curt slipped his arm around Kathryn's waist in proprietary fashion. "I'd like you to meet Mademoiselle Prim. This is her first trip to France and I wanted to show her the château. Jacques is our head vintner and a true master of his craft."

"Really." Still stunned by Curt's ownership of a vineyard, much less a hundred-room chateau, Kathryn smiled weakly. "How did he know we were here?" she asked under her breath.

"There's a phone at the back of the wine cellar. I called him when I went to get the glasses."

"Oh." If the man had waited a few minutes longer before arriving, he might have caught them in a very compromising position. Kathryn had been about to reject the need for a feather bed and plead for out-of-control passion on the dirt floor of the wine cellar instead.

JACQUES HOOKED UP the disabled Fiat behind his equally antiquated truck. As they bounced down the road, Kathryn sat in the cab of the truck, squeezed between Curt and the Frenchman.

For the moment, the misty rain seemed to have stopped, though the clouds still hung low across the rural landscape, providing a surrealistic backdrop to the evenly spaced rows of vines.

Within a few minutes, a massive stone structure appeared out of the fog. Three stories high, the château looked like a castle with a dozen chimneys peeking up through the slate roof, each corner of the building marked with a rectangular tower. A stray ray of sunlight slipped through the overcast and touched the square windowpanes across the front of the building like a magic wand, transforming the gray image with the same sparkle found in the most exquisite diamonds.

"Enchanting," Kathryn said on a sigh.

"Our plans call for turning the château into the ultimate bed-and-breakfast for lovers," Curt explained, his arm resting along the back of the seat. "We'll feature weekends here in the Seduction catalog as the perfect gift for when all else fails."

"You might want to consider paving this road. Otherwise you're likely to have a junkyard full of rental cars with broken axles. Not to mention a good many lovers with sprained backs."

He chuckled and gave her a quick hug. "Maybe I should hire you as a consultant. The female point of view, you know."

"Thanks, but I already have a job. Assuming I can get back to L.A. before Tom fires me."

BY THE TIME Kathryn had toured the great rooms of Château Amour and began investigating the spacious bedrooms, she was ready to concede that Seduction Incorporated would have a real moneymaker in the place. Even with most of the furniture covered with dust cloths, the château had a romantic feeling, as though this were the original home of Sleeping Beauty. It would be hard to resist a man's advances in such an enchanted place.

Not that Kathryn wanted to, she mused with a half smile. The feather bed Curt had touted so proudly looked quite inviting.

"You want to give it a try?" he asked.

"Do we have time? Cannes is still a long drive—"

He placed a quieting finger on her lips. "In France, there's always time for love."

She opened her mouth and tasted him with her tongue. Who was she to argue with such ancient wisdom when her body was already thrumming with desire?

Leisurely they undressed each other, taking time to admire the intimate landscapes revealed when each garment was set aside. Kathryn explored the rugged expanse of Curt's muscled chest, while he investigated the smooth mounds of her breasts and the valley between them. With growing familiarity, she surveyed that part of Curt that could fill her so completely. In return, her thighs learned the thrilling pleasure of his rough cheeks against her sensitive skin.

Together they lay down on the feather bed and Kathryn felt as if she was sinking into a sea of sensations. Enveloping warmth. Air redolent with the tangy scent of sex. The salty flavor of Curt on her tongue. The murmur of words of love in her ears. Buoyed by the utter softness of the mattress, Kathryn welcomed Curt's tender invasion of her body.

With the joy born of shared intimacy, they scaled the heights of intimacy. As one, they peaked, then toppled from the parapets to seek a closeness that only comes with familiarity.

AN HOUR LATER, dressed once again, they reluctantly stepped out of the château and walked down the steps toward the waiting car.

A man appeared without warning. A man with a camera.

Kathryn turned her head and tried to cover her face as the flash went off, a lightninglike reminder that reality was inescapable and never far away.

"Curt!" she cried.

"I'll get him." Grimly he took off in pursuit of the fleeing photographer.

Chapter Thirteen

Curt sprinted between rows of grapevines. He'd do anything to protect Kathryn—climb the highest mountain, swim the widest river, even slay a hundred dragons, if need be. He wasn't going to let one sleazy member of the paparazzi ruin her reputation when it meant so much to her. *She* meant that much to him.

For an over-the-hill has-been, Bernie Zimmer was quick on his feet. But Curt was younger and lots more motivated.

He dived after the fleeing photographer and clipped him at the knees in a perfect open-field tackle. The guy went down hard, his camera bouncing out of his hands. Curt got the creep in a hammerlock, his forearm pulling hard against Zimmer's throat.

"Leave off, Creighton," Bernie choked. "I'm just doing my job."

"Not anymore, you're not. Now you're working for me." He tightened his grip around Bernie's neck. Normally Curt wasn't a violent man. For Kathryn, he realized, he'd be anything necessary in order to defend her. "I'll double…triple what you'd get paid for those pictures. But I want the film and I want you off my back. Forever. And nobody hears from you that the lady and I were ever in France. Got that?"

"There's a thing called freedom of the press, man." He coughed. "You can't gag me."

"Can't I?" Curt brought his mouth real close to Bernie's ear, so close he could smell the guy's sweat. In a taut whisper he said, "Remember those tabloid stories that said I had connections to the mob?" Lies that had really gotten under Curt's skin, but he wasn't beneath using them now to persuade the photographer to mend his ways.

Bernie nodded.

"Think about that while I remind you the mob plays for keeps. Broken kneecaps happen all the time. Or if you'd rather, a phone call can get you fitted for cement shoes and a walk across the bottom of the Atlantic. What's it gonna be?"

He flipped Bernie onto his back and fisted his shirt tight against his throat. Red faced, the whites of his eyes were showing and his neck veins distended. "Or maybe I ought to just take care of everything myself," Curt threatened. "That'd give me real pleasure."

Bernie shook his head. "You can have...the film. No charge."

Curt eased his grip. He was shaking almost as much as Bernie, and his breath was coming just as hard. But the creep had bought his phony story about the mob. That's all that mattered—keeping Bernie scared speechless, at least as far as any tabloid stories were concerned.

"I like to pay for services rendered," Curt said. He shoved himself away from the photographer, retrieved the camera and exposed the film. "I like to know my employees are loyal to me and not to anybody else, like some flea-bitten editor who wouldn't know an honest story if one hit him in the face."

He whipped some bills out of his pocket and tossed them on the ground in front of Bernie, who eyed the money uneasily.

"Go on. Take it. And get outta here before I decide to break your kneecaps myself."

"Yeah. Right. I'm gone, man." Rubbing at his throat, he picked up the money and struggled to his feet. "No sweat, Mr. Creighton. Whoever asks, I never saw you."

"If I see a word in print about this trip, you know what will happen, don't you? It's a hell of a long walk back to the States underwater."

Bernie's head bobbed up and down like one of those toy dolls stuck in the back window of an old car.

"Beat it," Curt ordered. "And don't let me catch you skulking around again."

Taking a few steps backward, Bernie edged down the row of grapevines, then turned and fled toward the road.

Curt exhaled the breath he'd been holding. He had to steady himself by leaning against a vine-covered post. This business of bluffing a guy with threats to his life was no easy trick. For Katie, though, it was worth the price.

Making a futile effort to brush the mud from his shirt and slacks, Curt made his way back to the château.

Katie questioned him with troubled eyes.

"He's gone and I've got the film. He won't bother us again."

"How can you be sure?" she asked.

"Let's just say ol' Bernie and I had a heart-to-heart chat. From now on there'll be one less paparazzi dogging my steps."

Kathryn wiped a streak of mud from his cheek with her fingertips, wishing she could eliminate the sadness from her heart as easily. The realization that dreams have to end had suddenly struck home. "Are you hurt?"

"Who? Me? The original superjock?" His smile was a weak imitation of his usual heart-stopping grin. "Give me a couple of minutes to clean up and make a few phone calls. By the time I'm through, this trip of ours will have been erased from living memory."

"Erased?"

"Completely forgotten. The press will be able to dig all they want, but this weekend in France won't have happened. You weren't here and neither was I. Not driving around in a limousine. Not at the hotel or having dinner. And not here at the château. It didn't happen." He gazed at her so intently, and she wondered if he was feeling regret for the weekend...or for the fact they would have to deny they had shared the most romantic, passionate weekend she could imagine. "No one will be able to link our names together, Katie. I promise you that."

Kathryn knew she should be pleased by Curt's efforts to keep her name and picture out of the tabloids. And she was. But that didn't mean *she* would ever forget this weekend with Curt. Each moment was indelibly etched in her memory and would always be there when she needed to remember what it was like to freely love someone...and be loved in return.

But now the dream was over. Kathryn couldn't possibly live in the fishbowl that delineated Curt's public life. Because of his position and wealth, she doubted the press would ever allow him the kind of privacy she needed as a barrier against prying eyes.

THERE SEEMED LITTLE to say on the tiring flight back to Los Angeles, and even less conversation occurred during the taxi ride to Rudy's hospital. Contemplating her future consumed all of Kathryn's energy.

"What do you mean, we aren't going to see each other again?" Curt demanded in a low, angry voice.

Kathryn hurried down the hospital corridor toward Rudy's room, making a real effort not to let any part of Curt's body brush against hers. Not even accidentally. The resolve she'd so carefully, thoughtfully made on the flight home would be too easily shattered if he were to touch her once again.

"Last time I checked," she said, "you had a pretty good grasp of the English language. We're going to see Rudy, hopefully have a chance to meet Antoinette and then we're going to go our separate ways."

"No." He snagged her by the arm. "After what we had together in Paris—"

She whirled on him, her body responding in unwelcome, heated ways to the feel of his hand. "Don't you remember? The weekend didn't happen. It was all an illusion. And it's better that way."

"Why? Tell me why, damn it! We can work things out. I won't let them put your picture in the paper."

He was in her face, so close she couldn't look away, couldn't breathe without filling her nostrils with his spicy scent, couldn't think, yet she knew she had to remain clearheaded.

"How can you guarantee that, Curt? By paying off every photographer in the country? Nobody has that much money."

She wrenched herself free of his grasp and shoved through the door to Rudy's room. There was no possible way Curt could understand. Only a woman could comprehend the pain of being the subject of vicious gossip—the vindictive words that flayed a person's soul, the mean-spirited conversations that placed a lasting brand on a person's spirit. As much as she might wish it were otherwise, Kathryn simply couldn't put herself in that position again.

The tender scene she discovered in the hospital room easily excused the tears in her eyes.

"Madame Bilou?"

The older woman had to force her loving gaze away from Rudy to respond to Kathryn's greeting. In spite of her silver hair and a face laced with wrinkles, there was a youthful glow to Antoinette's cheeks, as one might expect when a woman of any age was in love.

"My dear," she said. "You must be Kathryn. Rudy has told me so much about you and I am so grateful..." Without finishing her thought, she extended a slender, veined hand across the hospital bed. "*Merci*. For being his friend. For making it possible for me to be at his side when he needed me."

Awed by the frail delicacy of the woman, Kathryn said, "Actually, it was Curt's idea and his plane. I can't take the credit for bringing you to the States so quickly."

She nodded graciously, then shifted her attention to Curt.

With European panache, he bent over the back of Antoinette's hand, brushing a kiss. "*Madame,* now that I have seen you, I can understand why Rudy has waited for you all these years."

A flush rose up her cheeks. "You are most kind, young man."

Kathryn leaned over to kiss Rudy on the cheek. "How are you?"

"Never better, my *chérie*. My Annie, foolish woman that she is, has consented to marry me when I am released from the hospital. The doctors say we will be able to set the date soon."

"I'm happy for you, Rudy. For both of you." She fought the painful press of tears that threatened to spill over onto her cheeks. *A chance lost is one you may never have again.* After all these years, Rudy and Antoinette were lucky to have found each other. Kathryn didn't expect she'd be given a second chance with Curt. Yet abject terror of what others might think, of what being in the spotlight would mean, imprisoned her as surely as the bars of a cage.

"We want you to be there, *chérie,*" Rudy said. "When we marry."

"I know no one else in America," Antoinette admitted, almost shyly. "I would hope you would stand with me?"

"Of course." Emotion thickened in Kathryn's throat. "You two need to have some time together. I just wanted to be sure..."

Kathryn couldn't deal with such overwhelming happiness, such enduring love. She bolted from the room on a wave of panic. She was going to lose Curt. Her heart was breaking, yet she couldn't face what loving him would mean. With all of his wonderful attributes, he was still a millionaire playboy, the apple of the tabloid's eye. She couldn't change him, and wouldn't if she had the chance.

He caught up with her halfway down the hallway.

"You can't leave. Not like this," he insisted, keeping pace with her hurried footsteps. "I won't let you."

"You're too bossy, Creighton. You ought to do something about that irritating habit." She kept on walking, her eyes straight ahead, praying he wouldn't stop her with his hand, or a soft word, because she wasn't sure she could resist his magnetic personality, his overpowering masculinity. Not when she wanted to bury herself in his embrace, forget the reasons why they had no future together.

He planted himself in front of her. "Where are you going?"

"I'm . . . I'm going to see my father." She looked up at Curt with an expression she knew was stunned. She didn't know where those words had come from, yet she knew they were true. The time had come for her to face her past.

"I'll come with you."

She shook her head. "I have to do this on my own."

His hand slid along her neck and his fingers wove into her hair at her nape. "You don't have to do this alone. I can be there for you."

"Not this time, Curt."

"Afterward . . . what about us?"

"I don't know," she admitted, vacillating between wanting to follow her heart and knowing she ought to listen to the warnings in her head. "I simply don't know."

"A few minutes ago you were giving me a straight no. I'll take a maybe as an improvement."

She wrapped her fingers around his wrist. "I can't make any promises, Curt."

He lowered his head, crushing her lips with a kiss he hoped she'd remember for a long time. Loving someone was harder work than he had anticipated. He had to let her go even though every instinct in his body shouted at him to never let Katie out of his sight.

He tasted the sweet flavor of her mouth and let her taste him, hoping this kiss wouldn't be their last. She was right to recognize that some things simply couldn't be bought. She was one of them. Yet he'd willingly give her every dime he had if she would be his.

With matching sighs, they broke the kiss.

"You'll call if you need me?" he asked, surprised he could find his voice past the thickness in his throat.

She nodded, but without a great deal of conviction.

"I'll wait." For as long as Rudy had waited for his Antoinette, if he had to.

With a small sound that might have been a sob, Kathryn slipped from his grasp and hurried down the corridor.

Curt waited for a few minutes, holding on to some crazy hope she'd reappear through the door she had just exited. He closed his eyes and pictured her in Paris. Her beautiful smile, her excitement. The way her hair had caught the rays of the setting sun. The passion with which she had made love.

God, but he wanted a chance to have a thousand more weekends like that—in Paris, or London, or New York. Even right here in L.A. It didn't matter where, as long as he was with his sweet Katie.

When Curt finally left the hospital, he was met in the parking lot by Tom Weston and two uniformed police officers. A shimmer of unease sped down his spine.

"What's up?" he asked his attorney.

"Just do what this officer tells you, Curt. Don't say *anything* without me being present and I'll have you out on bail as soon as I can."

BY THE TIME Kathryn crested Gorman Pass and headed down into the San Joaquin Valley, she missed Curt desperately. Flying along the highway, she ached with wanting him. As she passed almond trees that had dropped their leaves in gentle mounds of gold that stretched the length of the orchards, she thought about Curt's infectious smile, the way his cheeks creased and how his eyes sparkled with amusement...or darkened with passion. She remembered his wit and charm.

Traveling the main street of Waverly she tried to conjure up the faces of the boys she had dated, but the only image that came to her was Curt. He was no groping, fumbling adolescent who made love as if it was a speed race. With Curt, time was endless, a series of wonderfully weightless moments that blurred into a cloud of sensual delight. He had loved her with practiced skill, almost with reverence. Her every erogenous zone had been explored by him with precise accuracy.

And she knew him almost as well.

He was funny and smart. He offered shelter to wannabe starlets and kept a factory open in a small town in Alabama for sentimental rather than profitable reasons, honoring his mother's memory. He liked to fly kites and drive fast. He was, quite simply, a good man. Probably the best she'd ever met.

And darn it all, she loved him.

She'd never felt anything more strongly than she did the empowering emotion of her love for Curt.

It didn't much matter what anyone else thought, or if every time she glanced at a tabloid she'd see her own face staring back at her. She wasn't going to sneak around trying to hide her relationship with Curt. Let others gossip all they like. She was going to love Curt Creighton for as long as he wanted her. She only hoped it would be for a lifetime.

But the truth was, she realized with considerable trepidation, she didn't know how Curt felt about her. So much of the time his attitude seemed cavalier, that of a confirmed bachelor playboy. Yet she'd seen glimpses of his more serious side, that part of his personality that was even more appealing than his sexy grin.

A long time ago she'd been misled by guys who whispered a few sweet words in her ear...and by her own need to be loved. Curt's whirlwind efforts to seduce her might offer no more commitment than an adolescent's inexperienced gropings.

Dear God, how would she ever know for sure?

THE IVY-COVERED HOUSE where Kathryn had grown up was two blocks from Main Street, the biggest home on the block. She remembered how carefully her mother had tended the garden and her father's pride of ownership, the way he'd repainted the white trim around the windows almost every year. After her mother's death, Kathryn's father had seemed so distant, so unable to give her the love she needed that she had foolishly searched elsewhere. Maybe he'd always been that way. Or maybe, she considered for the first time, he'd been dealing with his own grief and simply didn't know how to handle a teenage daughter.

She pulled her VW Rabbit into the driveway beside the old weeping willow tree that shaded the house. Taking a deep breath, she headed for the porch.

The screen door burst open and a young woman with strawberry-blond hair appeared. A youthful twenty-five-year-old, she hesitated at the top step. "Kathryn?"

"It's me, all right. Your prodigal sister home at last." Smiling, she opened her arms wide. How she'd regretted leaving her sister when she'd been young and motherless, and wouldn't have if their father hadn't barred her from the house. "My goodness but you've grown up, Alice. Whatever happened to your braces?"

With a laugh, Alice flew down the steps and into Kathryn's embrace. "And what happened to those tight jeans and those awful cutoff tops you used to wear that gave Dad such a fit? In that suit, you look like you just stepped out of a corporate board-room."

"It's my dress-for-success look so I can impress Dad. I outgrew those particular jeans years ago." She'd outgrown a lot of things, Kathryn realized, without even being aware it had happened. Most importantly, she'd outgrown her need to please her father, or even to rebel against his dictates. She was finally her own person—and hoped her father could accept her that way.

Perhaps the seed of her independence had been planted when she'd been forced to go out on her own. Surely the roots had grown through all the struggles Kathryn had faced. But it was Curt, she realized, who had finally allowed the seed of self-assurance to bloom. How odd, now that she had found a full measure of self-confidence as a woman, she would need Curt all the more, knowing she was finally a match for him.

After she and Alice had thoroughly scrutinized each other, Kathryn asked, "Where's Dad?"

"Inside. He's been a nervous wreck ever since you called to say you were coming. I think he's scared."

"Scared?" Kathryn was the one who had spent years frightened of this moment. Until now.

Alice nodded. "Afraid you're still mad at him, I suppose."

She hooked her arm at her little sister's elbow and they walked up the steps together. "No, not mad. Not anymore."

He was standing in the entryway—thinner than she remembered, his long-sleeve sport shirt hanging from narrow shoulders. The gauntness in his face emphasized his Roman nose. What little hair he had left was almost solidly gray. He'd grown old while Kathryn had been away, and she could see years of regret etched in the lines of his face. *Opportunities lost.*

"Daddy." The word caught in her throat.

"I'm sorry, Kathryn. I'm so very sorry."

Relief cleansed years of hurt like a wave washes away unwanted debris from a beach. "It's all right, Daddy. Everything's all right."

"You weren't gone a half hour before I realized how wrong I'd been to send you away. I went looking for you. I scoured this whole town. You'd vanished. Thank God..."

Through the blur of her own emotion, Kathryn saw the tears in her father's eyes before he hugged her. He wasn't the intimidating man he used to be. Or maybe she'd grown up enough to accept her father with all of his human frailties. Still, it felt good to have his loving arms around her again after all these years.

THEY TALKED LONG PAST midnight—about Alice studying to get her secondary teaching credential at Fresno State University and having a gentleman friend who owned his own business, about the financial problems facing a local bank, and about Kathryn's work and law-school studies. They talked about the baby she'd given up for adoption and where she might be.

Sometimes they laughed. A couple of times they cried. Mostly they tried to relive the past twelve years in a single evening.

The next morning, Kathryn's father and sister were already eating breakfast when she got up. As she poured herself a cup of coffee, she glanced past her father to the television.

To her surprise, the familiar face of Curt Creighton, looking grim and haggard, gazed back at her. For an instant she thought she was hallucinating.

"...millionaire playboy has been arrested," the announcer said.

She turned up the volume.

"What's wrong?" her father asked.

"I need to hear this."

"The alleged attempted rape and brutal beating of Ms. Kellogg is said to have occurred over the weekend, although no specific details have been released as yet. Through his attorney—" a picture of Tom Weston flashed on the screen "—Mr. Creighton has denied the allegations but has not offered an alibi as to his whereabouts during the time in question. In a recent court case, Ms. Kellogg—"

Kathryn snapped off the TV. "That woman's crazy! Nobody will believe Curt would do a thing like that. He wasn't anywhere near—"

"You know Curt Creighton?" Alice asked, her voice excited. "A guy with that much money? And a hunk, too?"

"Not only do I know him, I'm his alibi. We spent the weekend together." She felt an instant punch of unease as she glanced at her father, worried about his disapproval, then shrugged off the sensation. Old habits die hard.

"Wow!" Alice exclaimed. "You've come a long way, Sis. Where were you?"

"We were in France helping out a friend." But, she suddenly realized, Curt had fixed it so their trip would be darn hard to prove. Obviously he was trying to keep her name out of the paper or he would have already offered his alibi. In the process he was jeopardizing his freedom. If that wasn't proof of his love, she didn't know what would be.

"Wait till I tell my friends—"

"Kathryn," her father said in warning. "If you step forward as this Creighton fellow's alibi, your name may well be linked with a lot of negative publicity. It won't do your legal career any good."

She set her coffee cup on the counter. "Dad, he's innocent. Surely you wouldn't want me to stand by and let an innocent man go to jail."

"I was only thinking of your future."

She patted her father's hand. *This* time she wasn't going to worry about what anyone else might think of her. "If I have my way, Curt Creighton *is* my future."

Chapter Fourteen

"Sorry, lady. You can't go in there."

"I'm Mr. Creighton's attorney," Kathryn announced in her most professional tone as she headed toward the door that permitted entry to the jail cells. Not breaking stride, she flashed a very impressive-looking library card in the police officer's direction. With any luck the young man wouldn't notice the significant absence of anything official about the ID.

"He's not there."

She all but skidded to a stop. "Where is he?"

"Upstairs. He and his *real* attorney are talking to the chief of detectives." He grinned at her. "You reporters are a real case. You're about the tenth would-be lawyer who's shown up this morning. Along with three mothers, two sisters and about five phony wives. Why don't you leave the poor guy alone?"

"No. You don't understand." *Five wives?* Not if she had anything to say about it. "I'm Tom Weston's assistant. He's the attorney of record and I'm his paralegal. He called," she lied, "and asked me to come down to the station."

"Sure, honey. And my name's Sylvester Stallone."

The heat of embarrassment mixed with fury, rose up Kathryn's neck. The man was so condescending it was all she could do not to fly across the counter and rake his eyes out with her fingernails. "What I just told you, Officer—" she peered at his name tag "—Officer Maloney, is absolutely true. You can call up to the chief of detectives, if you'd like, to confirm my story. And if you don't," she warned, leveling her eyebrows, "I'll have you up on charges of sexual discrimination, harassment and impeding justice. Trust me, it will cost you your job. Do I make myself entirely clear?"

Taken aback by her vehement statements and obvious anger, the young officer mumbled, "Yes, ma'am."

"Good." She nodded with authority toward the phone. "Then if you'll make your call to the chief..."

Minutes later it was Curt who appeared in the lobby. He snagged her by the arm and tugged her into a private corner of the room.

"What the hell are you doing here?" he whispered harshly.

"I should be asking you the same question. Since when do they let people under arrest wander around the police station?"

"I'm out on bail. Now tell me what you're up to."

"I'm here because I'm your alibi." *And because I love you,* she wanted to say, grateful that Tom had arranged for Curt's release so quickly.

"Don't you know the paparazzi haunt this place? I've got to get you out of sight." He dragged her to a doorway leading to the stairs, signaled the officer at the desk and hustled her through the door when the policeman buzzed it open.

The stale air in the stairwell chilled Kathryn. She shivered, as much because Curt looked so haggard as because of the frigid temperature. "You should have told them you were with me in France when the assault on Roz happened."

"Katie, sweetheart, nobody can prove where we were over the weekend. I did a hell of a good job erasing every sign of us being in France. If you stick your nose into this mess, you're going to get your face plastered all over the media. Not just the tabloids, honey. This is big-time news. You'll be prime fodder for both TV and the press." His hands formed concerned parentheses around her face. "I'm not going to allow you to put yourself in that kind of an unpleasant public position."

"I can prove we were in Paris," she said stubbornly.

"It's not possible, and I don't want you to. This mess will all blow over when they can't find any evidence to place me with Roz this past weekend."

She held up the rolled sketch they had made in front of the café in Montmartre Place. Knowing she'd have to have more proof than her word could provide, she'd stopped at her apartment en route to the police station. "The artist dated and signed this picture of me. I'd say that pretty well substantiates your alibi, along with my word about where we were. The police will have to drop the charges."

He looked at her with a stunned expression. His hair was rumpled, as though he hadn't slept in days. Her fingers itched to comb through the waves, to smooth them, to feel the sinuous sensation of silken strands caressing not only her hands but every part of her body.

"I'm not going to let you make that kind of a sacrifice," he insisted.

"If you stop me from telling the truth upstairs, I'll call a press conference on the front steps of the police station. I'll show this sketch to any reporter who will listen and tell them every detail of our trip to France. Well, almost every detail," she hastily amended, aware of the heated flush that crept up her neck. "At some point, the cops will have to let you go."

"Katie, you don't have to do this. It's my word against Roz's. They'll figure out she's lying."

"The district attorney is filing charges, Curt, and the case is bound to be a high-profile one. Trust me, there is no way to predict how a jury will react if they don't have all the facts. Besides, have you got something against telling the truth?" she asked.

"Of course not."

"Good. Then let's get upstairs and talk with the chief of detectives."

"Why are you doing this?" he asked.

Standing on tiptoe, she brushed a kiss to that spot where his cheek creased each time he smiled. "Because I love you."

Not waiting for his reaction, she slipped out of his grasp and hurried up the stairs.

Curt almost fell on his face in his effort to follow her. *Loved him?* God, he hoped his ears hadn't deceived him.

WITHIN AN HOUR Katie had the district attorney apologizing for ever having considered that Curt could be guilty of anything more than a speeding ticket. Shortly afterward, the police brought Roz down to the station where she tearfully admitted her boyfriend, Walter Simms, had beaten her, then threatened her with worse if she didn't go along with his scheme. A poor loser who held a grudge, Walter wanted another chance to tap into Curt's deep pockets. Not long after that, Roz was on her way to a shelter for battered women, with Kathryn's insistence that no charges be filed. She was, after all, as much a victim as Curt had been. Ol' buddy Walt was being interrogated by a very angry set of police detectives.

"Now let's get out of here," Curt insisted, taking Katie's arm. "There's an exit in the back."

"But the press is probably waiting out front." She veered in that direction.

"Yeah. Plus a phalanx of photographers and a half-dozen TV crews."

"Good. Does my hair look all right?"

"Katie, you don't want this. They'll eat you alive."

She smiled up at him with eyes overly bright with excitement. And anxiety, he suspected. "Does that mean my hair looks fine? Or should I take time to comb it?"

"You look gorgeous." No perjury with that comment, Curt thought. Katie's cheeks were flushed; her rapid breathing lifted her breasts beneath her tailored jacket in a way that made her look enticing rather than severely professional. A few strands of hair had escaped the loose bun at her nape and softly framed her face. She looked cool and sophisticated—and sexy as hell. No question, she'd wow them on the six o'clock news.

Only when she reached for the door did Curt notice that her hands were trembling.

"Oh, no, you don't." He halted her with an arm around her waist. This time she didn't resist when he pulled her into an empty hallway.

"You don't want to go out there and face that mob, do you, Katie?"

"I can do it." Her voice caught. "It's no big deal for me to have my picture in the paper. Even my dad will understand."

He lifted her chin when she didn't meet his gaze. Her eyes were glazed with tears. "That doesn't change who you are, Katie. You're still a very private person."

"But you're not. If I'm going to..."

With his thumb, Curt wiped a tear that had spilled onto her cheek. "If you're going to do what?"

"You need a woman who doesn't flinch under the constant scrutiny of the press. Someone who can wave and smile no matter what they print. I understand that and I want to be that kind of person for you, really I do."

Curt pulled her into his arms and hugged her hard against his chest. No woman on earth had ever wanted to change for him. She didn't want his money or any of the perks that went with it. She'd proved that more than once. She wanted *him*. And she was willing to put herself in the most painful position she could imagine in order to publicly clear his name. Curt felt awed by her courage.

"Sweetheart, did you mean what you said earlier about loving me?"

She nodded her head against his chest. "Yes," she whispered.

"Then why don't you let me decide what kind of a woman I need?"

"I can go out there, Curt. It doesn't matter if they gawk at me, or what they think. I'm a big girl now."

"Shh." Knowing everything she was saying was a sweet, tender lie, he pressed a kiss to the top of her head. There was no way Katie would ever be comfortable being harangued by the press. Frankly he was just as glad. "How 'bout instead of going out there, we issue a written statement saying we're engaged and we're going to get married as soon as humanly possible?"

She raised her head. "Married?"

He grinned at her surprise. "That's what people usually do when they're in love."

"But you've never said a word—"

"I think I fell in love with you the first time I saw you. But then I've always had a weakness for a crying woman. Or so Lucy tells me." He palmed her cheek. "Besides, if I'm an old married man with a half-dozen kids..."

She choked, but her broadening smile was irrepressible. "Six? We'll need to negotiate."

"...I figure the media will lose interest in me. That way I'll have more time to devote to my family."

"I suppose you'll tell me next you're going to take up raising corn and beans for a hobby?"

"I've already started. It's a good way to work out your frustrations."

She lifted mocking eyebrows. "I can think of a better way to get rid of frustrations."

Frowning as though considering her comment, while in fact he was fascinated by the enticing shape of her lips and the mischievous sparkle in her eyes, he said, "You're right. Maybe I'll let the back forty go to seed awhile longer."

She grinned. "You did just propose to me, didn't you?"

"I thought that was pretty obvious. I love you and I want to marry you. If you want, I'll get down on my knee. But it's going to hurt like hell on this concrete floor." He waited a moment for her response. When there was only silence, he asked, "You are going to accept, aren't you?"

"With conditions."

He sighed heavily. "You can be a very contrary woman, Ms. Prim. What conditions?"

"I'm sure LaVerne and LaVilla are wonderful young women, but they've got to go. And no more wannabe starlets are going to get a key to your house as long as I'm hanging around."

He tipped his head back and laughed aloud. "You've got it, sweetheart. From now on, you're the only woman in my life."

"Hey..." came a female voice from down the hall. "What about me?" Lucy objected.

Kathryn turned, embarrassed to be caught in a clench with Curt. She'd likely never get over this need for privacy, not after what she'd experienced as an adolescent. But with time, things would get better. They had already with her family, and she was looking forward to developing a closer relationship with both her father and sister.

"Not to worry, Sis. I don't think Katie meant you."

"No, of course not," Kathryn quickly agreed.

"I'm glad to hear that," Lucy said, tugging Tom Weston behind her, "because we've got some super good news. Tom and I are going to be married, and we want you both at the wedding."

Kathryn felt Curt's arm slide around her waist in a thoroughly, and totally welcome, proprietary manner. "In that case, Sis, maybe we can make it a double wedding."

Lucy squealed in delight. There were hugs and kisses and handshakes all around. A few tears included.

Finally Curt said, "Tom, you're going to have to go out there and deal with the media."

"Why me? You're the one they want to see, and you've got enough experience to handle a mob twice that size." He slanted a hungry, totally unprofessional look at Lucy, who was all smiles. "Besides, I've got something else on my agenda for tonight."

"Tough luck, guy. You're my designated mouthpiece. From now on I'm keeping a low profile."

"No!" Kathryn vehemently objected. She drew a steadying breath as the others stared at her in surprise. It was going to take a while to get used to being a media personality, but she would learn to put a damper on her bad case of nerves. "What I really want to do is shout it from the rooftops that I love you, Curt Creighton, and I'm going to be your wife. It seems to me that the best and quickest way to get you off the list of the top-ten most eligible bachelors in the world is to make our announcement right now."

"And let the rest of the women get on with their weeping," Lucy interjected with a teasing grin.

"Are you sure, Katie? We can still slip out the back door. I don't want to subject you to—"

She placed a silencing finger on his lips. "As long as your arm is around me, I'll manage."

Curt took her at her word. On the front steps of the police station, he announced their marriage plans to the world. Then he kissed her—long and thoroughly—and Kathryn wasn't even aware of the flashbulbs that burst from every direction. Or the laughter that turned to applause. She only knew she was in the arms of the man she loved and planned to stay there for a very long time.

THAT NIGHT, as Kathryn lay completely sated in Curt's arms, he said, "I think I've finally figured it out."

"What's that, dear?" she asked sleepily.

"Remember how I never knew what my father did that finally convinced Mother to marry him?"

She mumbled a sound that resembled a yes.

"As I recall, whenever they talked about Paris, Mother got kind of a dreamy look in her eyes. Like she was remembering an especially romantic trip they'd taken together." He gently rubbed his whisker-rough cheek on her forehead. "I'll bet that's it. Dad took her to Paris. Maybe they even stayed at the château and then he bought it for her. What do you think?"

"It's possible."

He snuggled her up even closer along the length of his body. "I'll have to pass the word on to our son when he's old enough. It'll give him a leg up when he meets the right woman."

"You do that, dear." She smiled a secret smile.

Maybe later—years from now—Kathryn would explain to Curt that he needn't have taken her anywhere. She would have fallen in love with his irrepressible charm right here at home. It was how he had tried to protect her, had been so concerned about even her irrational fear of publicity, that had really done the trick.

Meanwhile, she intended to enjoy as many trips to Paris as they could manage around the constraints of her studying for the bar exam and what she hoped would be an exciting law practice.

She'd mention that to their son, too. When the time was right.

Once in a while, there's a story so special, a story so
unusual, that your pulse races, your blood rushes.
We call this

NANNY ANGEL is one such book.

After one week as a single father, sexy Sam Oliver knows he needs help from the
Guardian Angel Nanny Service to care for his five-year-old daughter. But he isn't
prepared for the blond, blue-eyed out-of-this-world nanny who's about to land on
his doorstep!

NANNY ANGEL
by
Karen Toller Whittenburg

Available in February, wherever Harlequin books are sold.
Watch for more Heartbeat stories, coming your way soon!

Take 4 bestselling love stories FREE

Plus get a FREE surprise gift!

Special Limited-time Offer

Mail to Harlequin Reader Service®

> 3010 Walden Avenue
> P.O. Box 1867
> Buffalo, N.Y. 14269-1867

YES! Please send me 4 free Harlequin American Romance® novels and my free surprise gift. Then send me 4 brand-new novels every month, which I will receive months before they appear in bookstores. Bill me at the low price of $2.89 each plus 25¢ delivery and applicable sales tax, if any.* That's the complete price and—compared to the cover prices of $3.50 each—quite a bargain! I understand that accepting the books and gift places me under no obligation ever to buy any books. I can always return a shipment and cancel at any time. Even if I never buy another book from Harlequin, the 4 free books and the surprise gift are mine to keep forever.

154 BPA ANRL

Name _____ (PLEASE PRINT)

Address _____ Apt. No. _____

City _____ State _____ Zip _____

This offer is limited to one order per household and not valid to present Harlequin American Romance® subscribers. *Terms and prices are subject to change without notice. Sales tax applicable in N.Y.

UAM-94R   ©1990 Harlequin Enterprises Limited

He's at home in denim; she's bathed in diamonds....
Her tastes run to peanut butter; his to pâté....
They're bound to be together....

for Richer, for Poorer

We're delighted to bring you more of the kinds of stories you love,
in FOR RICHER, FOR POORER—a miniseries in which lovers
are drawn together by passion...but separated by price!

Next month, look for

#571 STROKE OF MIDNIGHT
by Kathy Clark

Don't miss any of the FOR RICHER, FOR POORER
books, coming to you in the months ahead—
only from American Romance!

HARLEQUIN®

A M E R I C A N ◆ R O M A N C E®

Four sexy hunks who vowed they'd never take "the vow" of marriage...

What happens to this Bachelor Club when, one by one, they find the right bachelorette?

Meet four of the most perfect men:

Steve: **THE MARRYING TYPE**
   Judith Arnold
   (October)

Tripp: **ONCE UPON A HONEYMOON**
   Julie Kistler
   (November)

Ukiah: **HE'S A REBEL**
   Linda Randall Wisdom
   (December)

Deke: **THE WORLD'S LAST BACHELOR**
   Pamela Browning
   (January)

STUDS

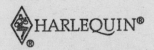

HARLEQUIN®

Deceit, betrayal, murder

Join Harlequin's intrepid heroines, India Leigh
and Mary Hadfield, as they ferret out the truth
behind the mysterious goings-on in their
neighborhood. These two women are no milk-
and-water misses. In fact, they thrive on

MISCHIEF & MAYHEM

Watch for their incredible adventures in this
special two-book collection. Available in March,
wherever Harlequin books are sold.

HARLEQUIN®

Don't miss these Harlequin favorites by some of our most distinguished authors! And now, you can receive a discount by ordering two or more titles!

HT#25577	WILD LIKE THE WIND by Janice Kaiser	$2.99	☐
HT#25589	THE RETURN OF CAINE O'HALLORAN by JoAnn Ross	$2.99	☐
HP#11626	THE SEDUCTION STAKES by Lindsay Armstrong	$2.99	☐
HP#11647	GIVE A MAN A BAD NAME by Roberta Leigh	$2.99	☐
HR#03293	THE MAN WHO CAME FOR CHRISTMAS by Bethany Campbell	$2.89	☐
HR#03308	RELATIVE VALUES by Jessica Steele	$2.89	☐
SR#70589	CANDY KISSES by Muriel Jensen	$3.50	☐
SR#70598	WEDDING INVITATION by Marisa Carroll	$3.50 U.S. $3.99 CAN.	☐
HI#22230	CACHE POOR by Margaret St. George	$2.99	☐
HAR#16515	NO ROOM AT THE INN by Linda Randall Wisdom	$3.50	☐
HAR#16520	THE ADVENTURESS by M.J. Rodgers	$3.50	☐
HS#28795	PIECES OF SKY by Marianne Willman	$3.99	☐
HS#28824	A WARRIOR'S WAY by Margaret Moore	$3.99 U.S. $4.50 CAN.	☐

(limited quantities available on certain titles)

	AMOUNT	$
DEDUCT:	**10% DISCOUNT FOR 2+ BOOKS**	$
ADD:	**POSTAGE & HANDLING**	$
	($1.00 for one book, 50¢ for each additional)	
	APPLICABLE TAXES*	$_____
	TOTAL PAYABLE	$_____
	(check or money order—please do not send cash)	

To order, complete this form and send it, along with a check or money order for the total above, payable to Harlequin Books, to: **In the U.S.:** 3010 Walden Avenue, P.O. Box 9047, Buffalo, NY 14269-9047; **In Canada:** P.O. Box 613, Fort Erie, Ontario, L2A 5X3.

Name: _____

Address: _____ City: _____

State/Prov.: _____ Zip/Postal Code: _____

*New York residents remit applicable sales taxes.
 Canadian residents remit applicable GST and provincial taxes.

HBACK-JM2